# Seaforth's Ladies: Revised Edition

Characters and Story Copyright 2018, 2020 Sandy Addison
Background and Technical Information Copyright 2016 By Clockwork Goblin and Warlord Games
Permission has been granted to the Author to use this material to create fiction works within the setting.
Image and Logo Copyright 2016 By Clockwork Goblin
Cover Art By Scott P. 'Doc' Vaughn
Published by Sandy Addison at Smashwords

**Smashwords Edition License Notes**
This ebook is licensed for your personal enjoyment only. This ebook may not be re-sold or given away to other people. If you would like to share this book with another person, please purchase an additional copy for each recipient. If you're reading this book and did not purchase it, or it was not purchased for your enjoyment only, then please return to Smashwords.com or your favorite retailer and purchase your own copy. Thank you for respecting the hard work of this author.

## Acknowledgements

The author wishes to thank Cliff A and Matt O for their long-time support and editing help with both this and other projects. One could not ask for better brothers both actual and figurative.

As I continue to explore what it means to be an independent writer in the 21st century, one of the unexpected pleasures has been meeting and working with other creative people. The first was Kira Omans (www.kiraomans.com) the narrator of the *Seaforth's Ladies* audiobook. I chose Kira to narrate the original Seaforth's Ladies because of all the potential narrators I had to choose from Kira was the only one with attitude, and someone like Alex needs attitude.

The second was Scott Vaughn (www.warbirdsofmars.com) the artist who created the wonderful cover for the revised edition. I've been following Scott for a number of years on Patreon and it was because of his Dieselpunk story *Warbirds of Mars,* that I approached him for my first commissioned cover. Like Kira he was a pleasure to work with, charged very reasonable prices for commissions and kept to his schedule.

Finally, a big thank you goes to Chris Hale (www.clockworkgoblinsminis.ca.uk) at Clockwork Goblin for allowing me to play around in his sandbox. If you ever make it out to Vancouver Chris; the first round is on me.

# Dedication

This book is dedicated to my mother Jean Addison. While she and Alex are of a similar stature Alex is very much her own person. Though it worried me as to just how close their characters *might be.* When I was describing Alex and her background to my mother. When I described Alex's habit of carrying a pair of brass knuckles and that it came from growing up in Steveston (where my mother also grew up); er reply was a very matter of fact 'sounds about right'.

# A Note regarding the Rank Spellings

As some readers may already know Lieutenant is pronounced as Leftenant within the British Commonwealth. As one of my ex-military friends put it. "Our officers *do not* manage toilets." In an effort to write a legitimate 'Canadian Accent' where Lieutenant is spoken by a non-American character, I've written it as Leftenant. In all other instances I've written it Lieutenant.

## Why a revised edition?

Generally, I was very happy with how *Seaforth's Ladies* turned out. Yes, there were some grammatical hiccups here and there, but this is an independently published book, and with editing costing an arm and a leg, such things are to be expected. I was spurred to go back to the story when I was editing the audio book with Kira Omans, and some of the questions she was asking. It was then that I realized that Seaforth's was a great little story for people who were already familiar with the *Konflikt '47* universe, but less so for someone coming to the story without knowing about the game. What did a Grizzly look like? What did a Thor? How did the war end up going on until 1947? It was then that I realized that I needed to add a lot more of the background that had gotten me interested in writing stories inside this universe in the first place.

This revised edition is an attempt to make Winnie's and his crew's story more accessible to the general public and hopefully inspire them to find out more about the world of *Konflikt '47* as a whole.

# Prologue

From *Walking into Germany: A Fighting Woman's Story* by Sarah May (1955)

In the spring of 1947, my personal goals were to stay alive, keeping my fellow crewmates alive and a grim determination to continue to grind the German's down and to finally win this war. While 'grind' wouldn't be the word of choice for many soldiers (certainly not Sergeant Mackenzie), I believe it best describes how the allies were winning. Even before defying my parents, to join the army I had taken an active interest in the war's 'big picture'. And the most amazing thing I'd taken from the war so far, was how much the allies had pushed back the Germans despite the lack of decisive victories.

I mean they tried, but time after time neither the Western Allies nor the Soviets were able to replicate the German victories like Norway, France in 1940, or early Barbarossa. Those early, battles of manoeuvre, successes made the German Army into a legend. While the allies could beat the Germans and push him back, we could never achieve a 100% victory. Take the Russian 'victory' at Stalingrad for example. They had that German army surrounded dead to rights, yet Jerry was, once again, with skill and sheer luck able to break through and get the army out. The Germans lost thousands of men and almost all of their equipment and were forced to retreat thousands of miles. Yet because the 6th Army survived the propaganda victory went to the Germans.

I think that's why President Roosevelt decided to go ahead with the nuclear attack on Dresden in March of 1944, before the Rift was fully understood. Here was a weapon that with a single use, or perhaps two or three, would end the European War; in a matter of weeks without millions having to die. That it instead gave the Axis the tools to fight us to a standstill and caused the great fracture of the alliance is what, I believe, broke Roosevelt, and caused him to decide not to try for a fourth term in office.

Looking back if there was ever one date that demarcated one era from another, both for the world and myself, I believe that date would have to be February 29, 1944. The day that the United States tested the world's first nuclear device in Los Alamos New Mexico. Not only did it mean that the United States had a powerful new weapon, but it was also on that date that a tear, a rift, in the fabric of reality formed and stabilized in the next several days. Unfortunately, the realization of what this Rift meant wasn't kicked up the chain of command in time, and Dresden was consumed in nuclear fire; with the same results as at Los Alamos. A tear in dimensional space. So now America and Germany both had access to their own Rift; and both were being contacted by group(s) unknown who said that they wanted to help them win the war.

Many have criticized the US for not capitalizing as quickly on the possibilities that Rift Tech offered them, as their German counterparts. I think it's fair to point out, that at the time, the allies were winning the war both in Europe and the Pacific. Whereas, the Axis powers were definitely losing, and needed something new to try to turn the tide. And, while we didn't know this at the time; the Germans were not getting exactly the same signals as the US was. Many of the technologies Jerry was being supplied with were easier to implement quickly. This combined with the willingness to put aside any ethical scruples resulted in the events in the Summer of '44.

The impact that Rift Tech could have in those early days had no greater demonstration than what occurred on both the Western and Eastern fronts in late July of 1944

On the Western Front; Operation Cobra had achieved its objective. A large breakthrough had just occurred, and Patton's Third Army was positioned to exploit the hole that the First Army had made in the German lines. In a perfectly timed maneuver, the Germans let loose the first of their Rift Tech weapons: The Zombie soldiers of the Totencorps.

When seeing obviously dead German soldiers coming toward them, many American troops broke and ran. Battle ready men fled in terror, not willing to believe that they were facing the dead. Those that did believe broke even faster, not wanting to face the 'next great evil' that the 'Satanic Germans' were going to unleash. For several days after the counter attack the number of psychological casualties outnumbered the physical wounded by more than 10 to 1.

At the Army and higher command levels, the reports from reputable officers and NCOs were viewed with disbelief. Not knowing about Rift Tech yet, rational men started to look for rational answers. Some sort of 'fear gas', mass hallucinations, or just plain old cowardice were all brought up as explanations. It caused General Patton to fly into a rage against his men, believing that they were all cowards. However, when Old Blood and Guts himself finally saw the 'Zombies' in action he was also hospitalized for 'battle exhaustion'. The line was only stabilized by a young artillery officer who believed what he saw, but was 'too busy to be scared'. He was able to convince his commanders to bring down the fire of every artillery piece in his Corps on a Totencorps attack and blew them into a million pieces. It was then that everyone realized that while Jerry might have had some new tricks, the Allies' massive advantage in firepower could still prevail.

A week later it was the turn of the Soviets to face the Totencorps. Like the Western Allies the Russian's offensive was stopped dead in their tracks just inside the Polish boarder. Stalin and the Soviet's high command response was swifter and more brutal than what occurred on the Western Front: they simply shot the men who fled. While this allowed them to get their offensive back on track faster, they had to do so without a lot of their best troops.

All through this time, the Americans had been playing the fact that they had, not once but twice, created rifts to another dimension, pretty close to the chest. Right from the start, only the very top of both American civilian and military leadership were being fully briefed; with the American allies only given the bare minimum of information based upon a 'need to know' basis. However, once the Germans had started showing the 'Dresden Rift' off in their newsreels the American's hand was forced. They confirmed to the world that the rifts were real and that *something* was coming through. However, they refused to confirm that any technical information had been gained from the rift with everyone but the British. This policy did not sit well with Stalin; who thanks to his spy networks in America, the UK and Germany probably had the most complete picture of the potential of Rift technology in the world. The Great Leader demanded American transparency on the issue. When he didn't get it, Stalin condemned the United States, stating that their direct intervention was no longer needed in Europe. The war against Germany was now to be a strictly European affair; though the Soviets still demanded the supplies they were getting from Lend Lease continue. When the Western allies called what they thought was Stalin's bluff in June with the invasion of Normandy, both London and Washington were stunned to get formal declarations of war from their former Ally. What had been a conflict between the Axis and a unified world had turned into a three-way battle for both the world and control of Rift Technology.

With the war taking on new dimensions, the race of technological advancements, which had always been heated throughout the war, became a complete inferno. Soon walkers, tanks on legs effectively, were being fielded by all nations still fighting in Europe. As were elite infantry units equipped with some form of power armour. However, all the major combatants were also starting to utilize Rift Tech in unique ways. The Germans; being the most desperate, created the most horrifying advances. Along with the already mentioned Totenkorps the Nazis started to mix human genetic material with that of various animals, creating the Schreckwulfen werewolves shock troops, and the vampire inspired Nachtjager terror squads. The Americans, inspired by their comic book superheroes, chose to enhance their volunteers in more subtle ways. Creating super soldiers that still appeared to be 'mostly' human. Thanks to their spy network the Soviets were able to steal both of these technologies creating their own hulking Ursus Bearmen, and Siberian Ice Ghouls, along with their propaganda winning 'Daughters of the Motherland'. Which in a perverse way I had to be grateful for. Without those female soldiers, I doubt I would have ever been able to crew Winnie.

The British decided to take their 'steel not flesh' doctrine, that they had since the start of the war, literally. Perfecting and then shrinking Turing engines to the size of a cricket ball the British started producing Automated Infantry, AIs or Alfreds for short. These eight-foot steel men started to replace the regular soldiers within the British and Canadian armies in early 1946. The Turing machines were also used in communications, allowing for a fast, encrypted communication net to be dropped over their entire battlefield. This allowed for even better coordination of their already formidable artillery along with armour, air support and other army assets.

Larger weapons were also deployed onto an already deadly battlefield. Tesla lightning guns are now being used alongside gravity cannons, force field projectors and magnetic rail cannons. Despite all these new and powerful weapons, all is still dependent upon the same Poor Bloody Infantryman, armed with a rifle, to take and hold the needed ground as they did at the start of the war. Only now he's got a lot fancier backup.

While it is easy to focus on all the changes Rift Technology had made on the battlefield, it is important to also note how it was being used on the home front. Thanks to their genetic experiments the United States had started to mass produce whole new lines of antibiotics and antiviral drugs, saving hundreds if not thousands of lives every day. They also produced an effective and safe contraceptive injection that women around the world welcomed. The Turing engines allowed for the creation of automated factories and mining facilities that opened up new lines of war production in the British Empire and Commonwealth. This allowed the Western Allies to keep up with the demands for new weapons and ammunition on all fronts of the war.

The German setup synthetic fuel refineries that not only allowed them to stay in the war, but also to reinvigorate their Luftwaffe and Kriegsmarine; making them effective fighting forces again. The Soviets got a hold of the plans for the Turing automated factories which allowed the Russians to replace the supplies lost due to the cancellation of Lend Lease. So, they were able to continue with as heavy a tempo of operations as they had before attacking the Western Allies.

Overall, this meant that the European battlefields of 1947 were far more complex and deadly when compared to those eight years before. Yet as I said before in some ways nothing had really changed. Young men, and a growing number of young women, still had to go out into that hell and fight. They weren't doing so just as regular infantry; but as modern knights in power suits that would have been the stuff of science fiction just three scant years ago. They were also manning tanks and walkers with more firepower than a platoon of tanks had at the start of the war. Yet still we went forth and with every fight, every battle, and despite the German's throwing surprise after surprise at us we kept moving forward. I knew we were going to win this.

It just took a lot longer than even I expected.

# Chapter One: Counterattack

As was their standard operating procedure, the German attack started with the screaming terror of the Moaning Minnies crashing down on the Seaforth's position. As the rockets hit, the quieter but just as deadly crump of the German 80mm mortars could also be heard as they hit with their usual deadly accuracy.

When the artillery bombardment had started, Alexandra 'Alex' Mackenzie had the unfortunate luck of being outside of her walker. She'd been making a much-needed call of nature at the first sound of the incoming rockets. Alex paused only long enough to pull up her pants before grabbing her captured StG44 and leaping into a nearby slit trench that her walker, Winnie, had dug just for this emergency. Only when she was in the relative safety of the narrow piece of dug earth did she take the time to do up the lower part of her uniform.

Her luck continued to be bad when, just as she finished, another body landed on top of her, pinning her in place.

"Williams! What the fuck?" said Alex; as she wriggled to get out from underneath the much larger man.

"Sorry Sergeant," said Williams as they both tried to occupy a space only meant for one person. Williams was a recent replacement, and while he wasn't lacking in courage, there was still a small town, United Church innocence about him. So, when his hand accidentally grabbed Alex's breast he immediately removed it with a quick 'Sorry Sergeant'. Unfortunately, that was the hand that was also supporting his weight so he once again landed on the petite NCO.

Alex knew it was impossible, but she was sure that Chantal and her other crewmates were laughing it up right now. "Stop squirming you idiot. That's an order!" she said knowing that the only way she was going to get out of this without cracked ribs was by taking charge.

"Yes Sergeant," said Williams in a deflated voice.

Alex listened to the artillery. Moaning Minnie attacks were intense but not continuous. The initial blasts in the area were done for now. They could now risk pieces of themselves being above the edge of the trench.

"Right; on three you're going to wriggle sideways towards your left," she said as she slapped William's left hand to make sure he knew which way she was talking about.

"Yes Sergeant!" replied Williams with greater confidence than before.

"Okay. Three!" said Alex and she also started wiggling to her left. With several embarrassing grunts the two Johnnies succeeded in changing places with Williams on the bottom and Alex on the top.

"Stay here until you hear the all clear call, we're in for at least one more rocket attack before the Krauts hit us with their ground attack," said Alex as she rolled out of the trench, reached back grabbed her German made assault rifle and ran towards her walker. Once she was by Winnie, the night started to get truly loud as the Corp's 5.5-inch cannons started their counter battery work and their own division's 25pdrs started to plaster potential concentration points for the German attack. By the time she had popped the hatch and got in the Winnie's cramped crew compartment, the second volley of Moaning Minnies was incoming. She got the armoured hatch closed just as the first rockets hit.

"Not as heavy as the first attack. Those thinking machines must have actually worked this time," said Lance Corporal Chantal LeBlanc, as Alex strapped herself into her seat. Winnie's driver's Acadian English was hard to understand to those unfamiliar with it, fortunately Alex and Chantal had been working together for four months and Alex had developed the ear for it.

"Yeah, well they can't be wrong *all* the time," replied Alex. She didn't trust a lot of the 'new science' that had come out since '44; except for Winnie of course, he was special.

"We've got company HQ on the horn," said Private Becky Popov, Winnie's Radio operator/loader, as the rest of the crew ran through the pre-start checklist for starting up the Grizzly Walker. They might have been under artillery attack, but it wasn't enough of an emergency not to keep to procedure.

Alex plugged in her headset and was quickly linked into the Seaforth's radio network, "Able Company this is Echo7Alpha we're up and ready," she said, her voice calm.

"Echo7Alpha this is Able. Be ready for anything including vampires," said company HQ.

"Roger that Able. We'll be ready," replied Alex.

Suddenly the Battalion CO himself was on the line, "All units! All units! This is Echo, attack incoming, repeat attack incoming. Light them up people and send the fuckers back to hell."

When the Canadians first started to receive the Grizzly Assault Walker, they did what they usually did with new kit: they tried to make it better. In the case of the Grizzly the improvements included the addition of smoke projectors. When the Germans started to regularly attack at night with creatures out of any sane person's nightmares; the smoke projectors had been converted to flare launchers, firing red magnesium signal flares to help light up the night.

At the call from Battalion HQ, Alex had toggled the switch which fired Winnie's flares towards the front. Soon six brightly glowing red flares were illuminating a fifty yards swath of land, one hundred yards in front of Winnie's position. Adding to this ribbon of light were flares from Able Compaines's 2-inch mortars and the Seaforth's 3-inch mortars.

"Tanks! Moving front, repeat tanks," said someone over the battalion's network.

Now that rockets had stopped, Alex risked popping the hatch to get a better look at what was happening. As she did so, Winnie lurched up onto his feet. He extended his arms and rotating his powered fists, he showed that he was fully ready for battle. Now they just needed targets.

Alex didn't have to wait long. Sure enough just as the first salvo of flares was halfway down to the ground, she saw several dozen large shapes loping towards the Seaforth's position.

"Gunner! Werewolves left ten degrees fire!" Alex shrieked over the headset. Even with the intercom Alex's voice was normally hard to hear over the roar of Winnie's engines. The only way Alex could reliably be heard was by loudly shrieking through the line, thus her nickname 'Shrew' by the other members of the Walker platoon when they thought she wasn't within ear shot.

Boom! Winnie's 75mm cannon fired its ready round towards the attacking Germans. In less than a second, a barely audible whump resulted as the white phosphorous round sent out chunks of the burning element, scorching German storm wolves, starting fires, and wrecking the werewolf's night sight. That the smoke combined with the flares to backlight the front line of the attack was just an added bonus.

"Gunner, load WP, adjust another ten degrees left," shouted Alex through the intercom's microphone.

"WP ten degrees left aye. Chantal! Rotate left," replied Sarah May, Winnie's gunner.

Alex held on to the hatch cover as Winnie's torso rotated left several degrees to help better align his cannon.

"Ready!" shouted Sarah. Unlike Alex, Sarah's voice punched through the walker's interior without amplification.

"Fire!" shouted Alex.

Another White Phosphorus round hit the German attack line adding to the confusion.

"Load HE, driver realign body to gun and prepare to advance on my order," Alex shouted as she pulled the bolt back on the 50 calibre M2.

"Loading HE aye!" shouted Becky as she rammed home another shell into the breach.

"Realigning body to gun," said Chantal as Alex felt Winnie lurch when his legs took two steps to realign its body to be in line with its cannon. He then squatted down lowering his profile but still ready for the attack.

"Fire!" said Alex over the com.

Once again Winnie's cannon roared: its high explosive shell adding to the chaos in the German's attacking force. As the Grizzly continued to fire its main gun, the platoon that the walker was assigned to also started to open up. Soon the ground between the two forces was alive with tracer fire as the five 'man' section of Alfreds opened with a mixture of Vickers and Browning heavy machine guns. Anything that made it out of the wall of lead and steel was immediately engaged by the two remaining sections of the platoon focus firing on the wolf-man super soldiers before they could get to friendly lines. The Canadians had long learned that German infantry would usually withdraw after they lost both their mad science weapons and whatever armoured units were assisting them in the attack. Therefore, Canadian rules of engagement prioritised the elimination of these components of the attack first.

Yet despite the Canadians' best efforts, several of the German genetically altered Schreckwulfen were managing to close on their defensive line. If the werewolves got into hand to hand combat none of the platoon, human or Automated Infantry would survive.

But Winnie was there too. Knowing what her commander was going to order before she voiced the command; Chantal had the walker rise to its full height and start moving to intercept the werewolves.

Whatever else the German scientists did to these men, they eliminated their sense of self-preservation, because three of the wolf-men attacked the Grizzly directly. Alex opened up on the lead wolf-man with the M2 Browning, expending half a belt of ammunition to literally shred the monster into blood chunks of flesh. Chantal shifted the arm controls and the large walker caught the second wolf-man in mid-leap as it tried to get at Alex. With a flick of her wrist on the controls, Winnie's steel fist started to rotate at high speed then suddenly stopped, breaking the creature's back. Winnie then slammed the dead body into the last Schreckwulfen sending up great gobs of earth and gore up into the air, crushing both creatures under the walker's 20 tons.

"Yeah! Show those bastards Chantal! Keep up the pressure. Bec: load AP we're going cat hunting," Alex shrieked into the intercom. With the werewolf attack stopped, for now, the young woman looked quickly from left to right trying to get a sense of the battle.

It was the chaotic battlefield that the young sergeant had become depressingly familiar with. The initial flares had died out but the battalion's 3-inch mortars were continuing to send more light onto the battlefield. Their glare was reflected by the smoke and dust from the white phosphorous, and high explosive artillery rounds and the dozens of small fires that they had started. Tracer rounds from both sides stitched the night in patterns that Alex had always found strangely beautiful.

"Echo this is Echo7Alpha wolves eliminated. Any more reports of tanks?" she said switching her headset to the company frequency.

"German armour attacking Baker's front. Permission given to all members of Echo7 for independent action," was the reply.

Alex switched back to Winnie's intercom, and barked out her next orders, "Alright ladies we've been given permission for independent action. Driver run towards the flare line."

Without thinking, Alex braced herself and she felt the Walker run towards what had been the engagement point of the German attack. Once past the illumination of the flares and fires, Chantal hit the Walker's headlights which though they provided very narrow illumination were enough to make sure that Winnie didn't end up breaking a leg in a polder or deep shell hole as it moved quickly through the enemy line of advance. A minute after they had started their one walker counter attack, Alex called a halt and Chantal put Winnie into a stalking crouch and killed the lights.

The feeling of being alone in an empty battlefield fell upon Alex as she scanned the night trying to get an idea of just where the German armour was attacking. Her search was suddenly made much easier by a bright explosion off to her left as what she assumed was a German tank suddenly brewed up.

"Driver left 90 degrees. Use that burning Panther as a target and guide Winnie in. Loader get up here and help guide Chantal, we'll keep the headlights off."

As Winnie stood up and rotated the direction that Alex indicated, the hatch next to Alex opened and Becky's head popped out of the Walker chassis. Becky, along with being the loader, had the best night sight of the crew. It was her job to help Chantal manoeuvre Winnie, keeping him out of obstacles that would break him or his crew. This allowed Alex to keep an eye open for 'human' threats.

"Alright Chantal can you see that burning tank about five hundred yards to your front?"

"Yes," said the driver.

"Good. It appears to be smooth sailing for now; open him up to halfway," said Alex

Once again, the large walker started to move forward through the night. Despite its size and the noise it made, the chaos of the battlefield offered the Grizzly enough cover that none of the Germans actually noticed them. Well that wasn't exactly true; the mortar platoon that they stumbled into noticed them. However, they could do little as Winnie ran through their position stepping onto two of the hated weapons as he went. As they left, Alex fired off a clip from her StG44 into the survivors to help convince them to keep their heads down.

Finally, Alex saw the German armour. Two of their remaining Panthers and what appeared to be an STG assault gun were crossing right in front of Winnie and his crew at less than fifty yards distance. Apparently, the Germans had satisfied their superiors' orders for a spoiling/terror attack and were now retreating back to their lines. The two tanks had rotated their turrets to face back towards the Canadian lines and were busy firing their cannons and MGs in the hopes of keeping the Canadian's heads down. Alongside the armour vehicles moved the remains of the infantry involved in the attack; despite their withdrawal the Germans' steel discipline still held.

As Becky dropped back down into her loader position, Alex got down to the business of destroying enemy property.

"Gunner target far Panther," shouted Alex into the intercom.

"Far Panther targeted aye," replied Sarah.

"FIRE!" shrieked Alex.

The sound of Winnie's 75mm roared out through the night. Its armour piercing round took the far tank square on the side armour and into the crew compartment. The penetrator cut through the thin side armour of the Panther and ripped through the tank's wet ammunition store, sending jagged metal flying around the tank killing most of the crew before they even knew that the walker was there.

The shot however, did get all the other German's attention. In seconds every German infantryman was pointing *something* at Winnie trying to let their armour know where the threat lay.

"Driver, body check that closest Panther. Loader, load AP," Alex shrieked again into the intercom.

The sergeant then involuntarily ducked as a Panzerfaust rocket went wide of the now moving walker. She gambled the same way every walker and tank commander had gambled since the war had started back in 1939. Do you keep your head out and direct your machine or do you button up?

This time Alex bet on keeping her head up and manning the Browning, sending short bursts of the machine gun's heavy rounds towards a knot of German infantry.

Then with a solid bang that shook the entire walker Chantal rammed Winnie's right fist into and through the remaining Panther's side armour in a perfect body check attack. The sound of the arm's hydraulics banging under the strain of the attack was soon drowned out by the screaming sound of nearly a foot of two-inch-thick steel armour being ripped from its mounting and then bent back as Winnie exposed the Panther's engine to the cold night.

Knowing what was going to come next, the Panther's crew leapt out of their doomed machine as Winnie backed off, allowing Alex to fire the remains of the Browning's belt of ammunition into the engine compartment. Sending high velocity bullets smashing into the large but vulnerable engine block. Piston cylinders were smashed and multiple fluid lines were ripped apart. Soon the pride of the Third Reich was ablaze like so much scrap metal.

"Driver pivot left bring that assault gun into line," Alex ordered as she held onto the Browning for dear life. Moving backwards at full speed to avoid the ill effects of an exploding tank while rotating the torso was a challenge even for a driver as good as Chantal. To do so without throwing the rest of the crew around like Raggedy Anns was impossible. While Alex did manage to hold on this time, she was still slammed hard enough into her hatch's side to see stars.

"Shit!" she said she fought to keep her mind present on the fight.

Seeing the 75 was roughly in line with the assault gun, Alex shouted "Fire."

Like any good gunner Sarah waited a second to get a clearer shot before she triggered Winnie's cannon. The capped armoured piercing shot caught the assault gun's front bogie wheel and ripped it off with ten feet of track.

"Time to get out of here ladies," hissed Alex still in pain from being slammed against the hatch.

"Chantal; show our ass and don't be shy. Becky; request Victor target on the green flare in front of Baker. Tell them it's Jerry's main line of retreat. Sarah get the cannon into the surrender position," Alex said as she reached down to grab the flare gun and the correct coloured flare. Returning to the hatch she fired the flare back towards the burning wrecks of the German tanks.

As they moved at speed back towards Baker Company's position, Alex rammed a fresh clip into the StG44 in case they ran into opposition on their way back to Canadian lines. Trying to reload the Browning while Winnie was running was next to impossible.

"Shit! Alex button up! Victor target request has been granted," shrieked Becky in a mixture of surprise and fear.

Without even thinking Alex slammed her hatch closed. She was stunned; she hadn't expected her request to be accepted; hell three years ago, lone tankers, couldn't have called in artillery requests. (Walkers didn't even exist yet.) But the same thinking engines that powered the Alfreds now monitored, filtered and enhanced the Commonwealth's radio web. One of those AIs must have agreed with her, because every gun and howitzer under 1st Canadian Corps control, over two hundred medium and heavy guns, were now zeroing in on the space that she and Winnie had left a minute before.

As shells started to land behind them Alex issued her last order before no one would be able to hear anything. "Loader, try and get a hold of Baker Company and let them know that we're coming in. Driver, surrender to our people."

Following through on her sergeant's orders, Chantal turned on every light that Winnie had and moved both of his arms to the 'hands up' position. Since German walkers, so far, didn't have arms this hopefully would be enough of a warning for the trigger-happy soldiers not to shoot at a friendly walker.

Realizing that for at least for now, there wasn't anything for her to do, Alex relaxed a bit and just let her crew do their jobs without interruption. It was then that the young sergeant had a horrible feeling come over her.

"Oh shit!" she said, not realizing that the intercom mike was on.

"What?" asked Sarah concerned.

"I have to pee again," Alex said with a note of frustration.

# Chapter Two: New Assignment

"But we've just been cycled back, for some R&R; why does the Brigadier want to inspect us now?" whined Sarah May, as she injected a fresh load of grease into Winnie's left knee joint. After coming off of the front line, it was 1st Canadian Army's standard operating procedure to do a rapid cycle of maintenance and rearmament to its walkers. Having most of the walker platoon ready to react to a German 'Terror' raid had saved the Seaforths, and the other battalions of the 1st Canadian Infantry Division, on more than one occasion.

"Because he's the bloody Brigadier and he can inspect the platoon any damn time he chooses," Sergeant Alex Mackenzie retorted as she helped their loader, Becky Popov, stow 75mm High Explosive shells in the Walker.

"I just hope he doesn't choose to inspect our personnel kits. I lost two pairs of silk panties when the divisional commander and his staff did their inspection," said Chantal Blou.

"That's because of the accent. You're exotic to everyone outside of New Brunswick," replied Sarah; she'd finished greasing the left knee and then turned her attention to the right.

"Either that or Chantal's panties were the only ones big enough for the old man to wear," added Becky knowing that she was out of Chantal's reach.

"Toton," cursed Chantal as she flipped the Ukrainian girl the bird.

"Ladies! Do not force me to put you two in the hospital again," said Alex before things got out of hand. Alex may have been the smallest of Winnie's crew but she grew up in Steveston, the hardest town on Canada's west coast and knew how to take care of herself; and like many sergeants before her, she was more than capable of taking care of matters with her fists.

Her two crewmates glared sullenly at each other but both kept their tongues.

"Alright then, I'm going off to see how the rest of the platoon is doing. Once you have Winnie ready, head to the showers. Corporal Smith and Sir Kay are going to stand guard. So, take your time and enjoy yourselves. This will be a full inspection so you know what that means: pressed uniforms, styled hair, makeup and shaved legs and pits. If anyone in the inspection party sees even a hair out of place, there will be hell to pay," said the sergeant

"And no swearing Sergeant you will have to remember that one as well," said Becky without even so much as a smile on her face.

Alex's face took on a neutral mask. Major Steves, the support company's commanding officer, had a thing about swearing in general and when it came to women in particular. Alex had nearly lost a stripe two months ago because the major had caught her swearing at the rest of the platoon after a poor performance in a training exercise. Leftenant Grassa had saved the situation with some clever political maneuvering. Unfortunately, that option was no longer available.

"I'd better see all the ammunition stowed correctly or I'll leave my boot sticking out of your rear entrance," replied Alex finally.

"Yes ma'am," replied the walker's loader with a big smile knowing that she'd just scored one against the bloody-minded sergeant.

Unlike their allies who deployed walkers in individual regiments like tanks, the Canadian Army had deployed its walkers as part of their infantry battalion's support company. Each battalion had a walker platoon of three sections; the 1st or heavy section consisted of two medium Grizzly assault walkers, while the 2nd and 3rd sections had two light Guardian walkers each. The Guardians were one-man units, whose main armament was a tempest flamethrower; backed up by several Browning machine guns. Why the walker had so many weapons always perplexed Alex. The driver could only handle one weapon system at a time so why have so many? That she even asked that question was most likely why she ended up with Grizzlies.

Unfortunately, two weeks ago, as part of a rescue attempt for a scouting patrol, the platoon had taken their first serious losses. They'd gotten the patrol out, but a hidden PAK 40 anti-tank gun had cost the unit a Grizzly and a Guardian walker. They had recovered the walkers and while the Guardian had been patched up and was ready to get back into the line, the Grizzly had been a complete write off. What hurt more though, were the two dead and one wounded from the engagement. That one of the dead had been 2nd Lieutenant Grassa had cut the entire platoon deep. The Lieutenant had been in command of the platoon since its creation six months ago and her death had left a big hole in the unit. She'd been the platoon's mother, taking care of everyone and everything and made it look so easy while she was doing it. As Platoon Sergeant, Alex had been trying hard to fill that hole but there was only so far that 'The Shrew' could stretch herself.

That the platoon was down two walkers made the situation both better and worse. While she didn't have as many personnel to worry about, the Battalion CO still expected the walker platoon to function at full effectiveness. As she approached the 2nd section, which now contained all three Guardians it was the section commander Sergeant Ida Vergamy that was first to see Alex coming.

"Ma'am," she shouted, jumping down from her Guardian and gave Alex a parade level salute.

Alex sighed, "Don't you start with that bullshit Ida. I'm not in the mood." Ida was the closest friend that Alex had in the platoon, but sometimes her attitude grated Alex nerves.

The other NCO lowered her hand and gave Alex a big smile her brown eyes twinkling with mischief. "Get used to it Alex, you're the platoon's commander. It's only a matter of time before they'll try and make a lady out of you, especially after what you pulled off two nights ago.

Alex groaned at even the suggestion that she could be made an officer. She liked being a Sergeant. Getting her hands dirty and 'just' commanding Winnie; she could handle that. But given that the alternative was a complete stranger taking over the platoon, she'd long ago decided that being in command was the lesser of two evils.

"How are the Guardians?" Alex asked as she walked past her friend to view the three light walkers. Since the Guardian only had a single crewman, Alex had ordered the platoon's entire maintenance crew (all three of them) to help with their rearming. She and Winnie's crew could get the walker back up and running faster without help anyways.

"Oh, pretty much up and ready. Unlike you and Winnie, we know better than to run into no man's land to take on the enemy after they showed the good sense to withdraw," replied Ida, her amused tone suddenly turning serious.

"If we hadn't, we would have been accused of not being aggressive enough, and that would have been used as a mark against having women as walker crews," replied Alex.

"Bullshit. You did it for the thrill. You're as addicted to the combat rush as much as any paratrooper. Do not use 'we have to prove ourselves every time we go out' excuse. Even the Leftenant wasn't buying that anymore," said Ida hotly; her Italian accent coming through toward the end of her rant.

Alex resisted the urge to deck her right then. Ida hadn't been there from the start; she didn't know how close things had been. "The Leftenant knew the score a lot better…" she started.

"And she's dead. And the only thing keeping this platoon together now is you. Did it ever occur to you what would happen to this platoon, to the entire idea of women in combat if you had died last night? Alex you're the toughest woman in this platoon; hell, you're one of the toughest people in the battalion. You do not have to keep proving that," Ida said hotly.

Alex was about to say something when she glanced around and saw that everyone in earshot was now focused on the two women. She cut back her remark suddenly remembering that she was at least for now in command of the platoon, and while Ida was a friend, she was also junior in rank to Alex.

Taking in a deep breath, Alex hissed quietly "This ends now. I will not tolerate being dressed down by a subordinate. Once we're back to being on more equal ranks, we will return to this discussion behind the showers. Clear?"

Ida, surprised and hurt by her friend's abrupt pulling of rank: stepped back and once again gave Alex a parade ground salute. Only this time there was no playful mocking to it.

"Those walkers had better be ready to fight since you're all standing around gawking," said Alex to the rest of the platoon, her voice breaking as she tried to shout the point.

The Shrew had spoken, and suddenly everyone became extremely busy.

"Sergeant Mackenzie!" shouted a voice from across the yard.

Swearing under her breath, Alex turned to acknowledge Major Steves as he moved determinedly towards her with a sharp parade drill salute.

"Why are you and your ladies, not getting ready for the inspection?" he said angrily. The officer was a short thin man that could have made a good walker crewman himself if he had wanted to. Instead he was a short man in a tall man's army who felt it was his right to take out his frustrations upon those who were both shorter and lower in rank to himself.

Only problem was that Alex wasn't having any of it. "Sir; we are sir," she replied.

"No, you're not. You're wasting precious minutes rearming your machines. This is why you women always need so much time getting ready: you waste time with things that can be done later," said the Major in a condescending huff.

"Sir, standing orders…" Alex started.

"I am well aware what the standing orders are Sergeant," Steves interrupted. "I am also aware that such orders are conditional depending upon the situation. And right now, the situation is that our Brigadier is going to be inspecting this company in less than two hours and your platoon is a disgrace because you are not using your time efficiently. I swear Sergeant if this platoon is not parade ready when the Brigadier arrives, I'll bust you down to Private and see how Sergeant Vergamy does in command. Now stop this pointless rearmament and get your walker ready for inspection. Oh, and the Company Sergeant Major tells me that you're late with the daily reports again. I'm surprised Sergeant, being a woman, I expected more from you regarding secretarial work.

"Yes sir, is that all sir?" Alex said through gritted teeth.

"Isn't that enough? But yes, that is it for now," he said as he turned and marched off to wreck one of the other support platoon's day.

Watching him leave, Alex waited until he was out of earshot before turning back to Ida.

"Sergeant, finish rearming the Guardians, and then get them ready for inspection," she said.

"But the Major said," started Ida.

"The standing orders are very clear and given by a competent superior officer Sergeant. Rearming and refueling all walkers coming off the line *is* the priority," replied Alex in the tone that she took when she was ready to hit something.

"Take command of the platoon Ida. I have to go finish off the daily reports," Alex said. They were already late but the excuse of needing to get them done would give Alex a chance to cool down before the inspection.

"Ma'am," replied Ida. This time there wasn't any mockery in her tone; just respect for having to deal with an asshole.

Alex headed to the Lieutenant's old tent to spend some time alone and to calm down. Steves's badgering always brought the worst out in her. Once inside she pulled out one of her precious bottles of Coca Cola and after draining half of its contents actually did try to get some of the endless paperwork done.

Pretty writing had never been a strong suit for Alex, however since joining the army back in '44 Alex had become reasonably fast at printing. As a result, she was actually able to finish her daily logs and after-action reports before she too had to head to the showers to get ready for the inspection.

Putting the logs, and more importantly her Cokes, back into the platoon's strong box for safe keeping, Alex got a runner to send in her reports to battalion HQ. Only then did she head back to Winnie's lager, collect her personal kit and then head to the camp's showers. As she approached, she could hear the sound of her platoon enjoying one of the few luxuries that they could get this close to the line: hot showers. Making sure that the women could enjoy this luxury without having to worry about several hundred men trying to catch a peek at naked female flesh stood Corporal Jane Smith of Able Company's Alfred platoon and 'Sir Kay' her Automated Infantryman. It had been one of the unwritten agreements among the growing, but still small, population of female soldiers serving in front line and close to front line units, that they would cover each other when showering.

"Afternoon Sergeant, better hurry they must be through most of the hot water by now," said the Corporal as she shouldered a large two-handed wrench.

Alex was about to say something back when Sir Kay actually gave her a passable bow.

"You teach it that Smith?" asked Alex taken aback by such a human action from the machine.

"What the bowing? Oh no Sergeant; he picked that one up himself after we watched those Robin Hood serials last week. Sir Kay is the best gentleman of the lot I'd say," replied the mechanic with pride.

"It at least knows how to keep its mechanic happy, which I imagine can't be said about a lot of walker crewmen," said Alex as she remembered the number of dirty looks, she gotten from her own mechanics when she brought Winnie in after a fight.

"Oh, he does that," said Smith patting the ten-foot monster on its hip.

"Well if you excuse me, I'd best take your advice and get in there before all the hot water's gone," replied Alex stepping into the shower area.

\*\*

Two hours later with bodies washed, hair curled, eyebrows plucked and the last of the precious Paris lipstick used, the women of the Seaforth Highlanders of Canada's Walker Platoon stood at rigid attention. Their combat boots were mirrored black, and their infantry battle dress fit perfectly, thanks to hours spent tailoring them. Behind the young women stood their walkers. Winnie and the three Guardians along with being fully armed, fueled and ready for battle had been washed and as many of the scratches and bullet marks that could be reached had been painted over.

"Jesus, they think they're in a fucking Guards battalion," said a new private in the mortar platoon when he saw how the women had turned out. The men of the support company had also taken advantage of the showers, and their appearance could be described as 'clean' if a person was feeling generous. To their credit however, all of their equipment was maintained and battle ready; and to any battlefield commander that was what was important.

Alex couldn't help but snort at the comment though. The men could get away with that attitude. They hadn't had to fight tooth and nail just to be allowed their share of the action. The Sergeant knew that there were still a lot of officers in the higher command who thought that women had no place in combat. This despite the Soviets deploying women fighter pilots, snipers, and those damned Daughters of the Revolution. Not to mention that it was a fact, not a theory but a proven fact, that women made better walker drivers because of their lower centre of gravity and their smaller size.

Still, as Lieutenant Grassa had driven home to Alex time and time again: all that it would take was just one SNAFU on any of their parts and everything that they'd won would be taken away from them. That SNAFU hadn't happened under the Lieutenant's watch and Alex had vowed that wasn't going to happen on her watch either.

Hence, the Guard's quality while on parade.

However, Alex wasn't the only one to hear the man's comment, all of Winnie's crew did. Fortunately, Chantal didn't rise to the bait and maintained her 'at ease' pose. Unfortunately, Becky and Sarah did take the bait. Sarah's response was simple; she flipped the man the bird. Becky's response was far more provocative for many, as she leaned back, established eye contact with the mortar crewman and blew him a kiss.

"No movement in the ranks," ordered Chantal. The Acadian had taken over Alex's role as the crew's disciplinarian as Alex 'played' at being platoon leader.

Chantal's order was mimicked by the Mortar's Platoon Sergeant. Unfortunately, where Becky and Sarah were smart enough (or just more afraid of what Alex would do to them) to instantly obey, the Private had other ideas.

"But Sergeant, did you see what that bitch did?" he said in a too loud a voice.

"Quiet in the ranks," hissed the Sergeant, as the Mortar Platoon's Lieutenant looked over to see who was causing problems right before inspection. Fortunately, the Private's friends quieted him before he said anything else.

Near crisis dealt with, both Platoons settled down and were ready in more than enough time for inspection.

\*\*

As the Brigadier walked down the ranks, Alex realized that this really wasn't the usual kind of inspection. First off, the Brigadier was accompanied by far too many people. Oh, the two Galahad equipped members of the Lone Scots, 1st Canadian Army's Headquarter Defense and Personnel Battalion were to be expected. Every commanding officer above the rank of Major had an escort of men in the powered suits now. Also expected were the Brigadier's several aides, and the Seaforth's Battalion Commander, and his aides. What wasn't expected were the two other Galahads bearing the insignia of the Coldstream Guards escorting a British Colonel and a British Female 2nd Lieutenant.

For his part, Brigadier David Sharpe was equally uncomfortable with this inspection but for entirely different reasons. He was a Permanent Forces officer that others would describe as an old school hard ass. But he was also, like most modern senior officers, a severe pragmatist. He'd had to absorb a lot of new things these past three years, the two biggest were now right in front of him: walkers and women walker crews. As he walked into line with Winnie his eye was drawn first to the walker. Although not as large as some of the German machines, up close the Grizzly walker class was still an impressive machine of war. All American designed Walkers were roughly man shaped with a torso, two arms and two legs. The Grizzly was armed with the same 75mm cannon present in the older model Shermans. It could fire a wide variety of shells and was still considered a very effective anti-infantry weapon. The two powerfists were also highly prized by their crews, being useful for everything from mundane tasks such as clearing obstacles and entrenching to tearing apart German bunkers and tanks. But then Brigadier Sharpe's gaze turned to the walker's crew. He was then less impressed and more amazed by what he saw.

Before him stood four girls, all of them appeared to be far too young to be in the army let alone in combat. Unfortunately, that was a pretty standard reaction for him anytime he reviewed any infantry unit nowadays. Most of the soldiers on the bleeding edge were too damn young. His reaction to the walker crew was perhaps more severe, due to how small they all were. The tallest was maybe 5'5" in her boots, while the girl with the sergeant chevrons was maybe 5'2". He couldn't reconcile the aggressive behavior that he'd read in the after-action reports with such a petite thing.

Though petite wasn't probably the right word. The Brigadier was more than willing to admit that there was little fragile about the red-haired sergeant. She projected a similar no nonsense, tough as nails air that he'd seen in all the good non-coms of any army.

"Sergeant Mackenzie isn't it?" said the Brigadier to Alex.

"Yes sir!" said Alex as she snapped the older man a perfect parade ground salute. Though she kept it out of her voice, Alex got very nervous. She'd been in the army long enough to know that it was never a good thing when a senior officer knew your name.

"I've read Leftenant Colonel Goodbar's report on your last engagement. Congratulations. You and your crew are to be Mentioned in Dispatches for your actions. Taking the offensive and destroying three armoured vehicles, not to mention your recognition of a proper Victor Target. That was well done for any soldier let alone a woman," said the Brigadier with complete sincerity.

"Thank you, Sir!" replied Alex keeping her voice low so that it didn't squeak with the increase of volume. The older man meant well, so she tried very hard not to show just how much the 'even for a woman' comment pissed her off.

Brigadier Sharpe decided that he suddenly wanted to know more about this walker crew. He took a step down the line coming face to face with a round face private whose dimpled cheeks gave her a cheerful disposition even when she tried to look serious. Despite himself the Brigadier started to smile.

"Name?" he asked, regaining control.

Again, with a perfect parade salute the private said "Private Becky Popov Sir!"

"And what do you do aboard that thing?" the Brigadier asked gesturing towards the walker.

"I'm Winnie's loader and radio operator, Sir!" replied Becky.

"That sounds like a lot to do," said the Brigadier innocently.

"The Sergeant likes to keep me busy: Sir," Becky replied with a ghost of a flirtatious smile.

'There's always one in every squad,' thought the Brigadier as he moved on.

Before he even asked, the next girl also gave a perfect salute and then said, "Private Sarah May. I'm Winnie's gunner."

"That was some excellent shooting private, keeping your nerve while facing enemy armour is not an easy thing," said the Brigadier, trying not to stare. She was easily the most attractive girl in the platoon with large blue eyes, clean lines to her face and golden blonde hair. It was also just as obvious with the large horn-rimmed glasses and severe bun for her hair, that she was trying very hard to downplay that fact.

"It was a team effort. Sir!" replied Sarah rejecting the premise that she was somehow more important than anyone else on the team.

Nodding approval to the very army answer, the Brigadier took another step down the line, so that he was face to face with Chantal.

"Well by process of elimination you must be the walker's driver," he said to the Acadian.

"Yes Sir! Lance Corporal Chantal Blou," she replied with just as good a salute as anyone else in the line.

"Leftenant Colonel Goodbar has been telling me you literally ripped one of the German tanks to shreds. Where did you get so good at beating up the enemy?" the Brigadier asked.

"I played hockey with my older brothers," Chantal said with no hint of sarcasm.

Once again, the Brigadier smiled, "I bet you gave as good as you got," he said as he remembered his own games of shimmy with his much larger older brothers, and all the bruises and bleeding lips and noses that resulted.

"I tried Sir," Chantal replied.

The two shared another smile, and then the Brigadier moved on to talk with Ida and the rest of the walker crewmen before moving onto to the other components of the support company.

"Well done Sergeant, your platoon has impressed the Brigadier," said Lieutenant Colonel Goodbar as he followed up behind the Brigadier.

"Thank you, Sir," said Alex a note of caution in her voice; something was definitely up.

"In fact, you impressed him and some other top brass so much that they feel you and your platoon is perfect for a special assignment. I'll explain more to both you and your number two later; report to my HQ at 1900 hours.

"Yes Sir," replied Alex, realizing that she'd just been 'volunteered' for something, which was never a good thing.

# Chapter Three: Lieutenant Johnson

As Alex entered the Seaforth's Battalion Headquarters, she knew that something was up. First off, the two Cold Stream Guards were still there in their Galahad armour, as were the two Lone Scots. That meant that both the Brigadier and the British Colonel were still here.

"What the hell is going on?" asked Ida; the dark-haired sergeant could read the signs of trouble as good as Alex.

"I'm not sure, but I think we're about to find out," replied Alex as a harried Staff Sergeant collected the two young women and ushered them into the Old Man's office. Sure, enough there was enough brass in the room to start a marching band, with Major Steves, Lieutenant Colonel Goodbar, Brigadier Sharpe, and the still unnamed British Colonel there along with two other majors (one British one Canadian) and the woman 2$^{nd}$ Lieutenant Alex had seen earlier. Military discipline was the only thing that saved the two as they moved into the room, saluted the Brigadier and then stood at rigid attention.

"At ease ladies," said Brigadier Sharpe.

"Sir," replied Alex, as both she and Ida 'relaxed' into an at ease position.

"Sergeant Mackenzie, given your record, and the lack of a commanding officer of the walker platoon, you would normally be a shoo-in for being brevetted to 2nd Lieutenant. However, right now you're more valuable to the Army where you are," started the Brigadier.

Alex tried very hard not to let the disappointment show, but she failed to keep it all off of her face. She thought that she had not wanted the commission, but with it being taken away from her, it suddenly felt more important than anything.

"I can see you're disappointed and bluntly I don't blame you. You're an aggressive leader who isn't afraid to take the initiative when necessary. We need soldiers like you in command positions," continued the Brigadier.

Those words did more to take the sting away than the Brigadier knew. Just soldier, not woman soldier, or female soldier; that one phrase alone meant a lot to the young woman.

"However, I believe that once you hear your part in a new test program you will understand why you were chosen," said the Brigadier.

"Sir?" asked Alex. Okay now she was curious.

"Ah. I believe that's my cue. Leftenant Colonel Goodbar, Major Steves, Sergeants, my name is Colonel Blastford. I'm part of His Majesty's Royal Personnel and Training Board."

Not waiting for a response, Colonel Blastford continued, "Your army's experiment with women in combat roles has caused quite a bit of stir at SHAEF. As much for its unorthodox approach to the personnel shortages were all facing, as the fact that it appears to actually be working. That success has caused pressure from certain members of all allied governments to at least do testing of our own regarding how to integrate women into frontline combat roles within our own military organizations.

"For His Majesty's Armed Forces these pressures have resulted in us currently retraining two all-female auxiliary antiaircraft batteries and the female components of a service and maintenance battalion into walker crews. The plan currently is to form a walker regiment, equipped with standard variety walkers; including our new Merlin heavy walkers. We're hoping to give the unit some seasoning by taking the graduates from our first female walker class and adding them to your army's replacement pool.

"So, the various battalion and support company commanders are going to do the dirty work of evaluating these crews and making the cuts for you," said Lieutenant Colonel Goodbar sarcastically.

"Exactly! As well, you and your Major Steves will have the additional pleasure of evaluating our Leftenant Johnson in her role as the new commander of the Seaforth Highlanders of Canada's walker platoon," Said the English Colonel. If he picked up on Goodbar's sarcasm he didn't show it.

With her name finally being used the young woman stepped forward and said to everyone present, in clipped high-class vowels. "I look forward to working with everyone here."

\*\*

Later that night the crew of Winnie sat down together in a local Dutch tavern that catered to the military personnel in the area. Along with the 1st Canadian Division R&R base, two small RAF forward air bases and a Dutch Army base were well within reach of the tavern by car so the place was packed with personnel from at least three different countries and over a dozen different branches of the military. The demand was so high for the simple reason that it was civilian owned. That meant real non-preserved food; prepared by cooks who hadn't been taught by the army; non-regulation alcohol that wasn't produced by the lowest bidder; and most importantly, girls who were actually impressed by a non-com's uniform.

Needless to say, the place was extremely popular with all the local military personnel. So popular in fact that you needed a special pass to get through the MPs at the village's edge let alone anywhere near the tavern. Alex and the rest of Winnie's crew had been given four of the special passes in part as a reward for being Mentioned in Dispatches and as a consolation prize for having to put up with wet nursing a new lieutenant and a Brit at that.

"Here we go ladies," said Becky as she put four glasses of Pilsner beer in front of her crewmates. She then turned to Alex and passed the sergeant back her $5 military scrip bill.

Alex looked perplexed; traditionally she always bought the first round whenever the crew went out as a group.

"The owner said that it was on the house in light of our award," said Becky with a bright smile she then added, "As far as I could tell, he was sincere and not shilling for anyone else."

"You sure," asked Chantal before she took a sip from the pale lager. All of the women at the table were well aware of the belief of many of their 'brothers in uniform' that buying a girl a drink created obligations later in the evening.

"Yes I made sure, though if it had been from those American flyboys over there I would have said yes," said Becky as she nodded her head to a group of five USAAF personnel. Even if they weren't wearing their wings, their swagger and attitude would have marked the Americans as pilots.

"How the hell did they rate passes to this place?" asked Sarah as she took a little too long a look at the yanks.

"Who cares, they're here. If they ask us to dance, I'm saying yes," said Becky, a little cheeky. She had never danced or flirted with American pilots and she was bound and determined to change that tonight.

"Why not go up and ask them to dance?" suggested Alex just before she took a sip of her beer.

Before Becky could explain yet again to her overly aggressive commander why asking men to dance wasn't a good idea, the Tavern owner's daughter Rivka came to their table and placed a large plate of Soused herring onto it.

"Umm Rivka we didn't order any food yet," said Alex.

"It is a congratulations for your reward by the army. We just got a fresh batch in from the capital and you are certainly entitled to the first order," said Rivka earnestly. The blonde Dutch girl then gave them all a curtsy and left.

A large smile broke out onto Chantal's face as she grabbed one of the lightly pickled raw fish by the tail and proceeded to eat it Dutch style in one piece.

"And she wonders why she can't get a date," said Becky as she watched her crewmate devour what the Dutch considered to be appropriate pub food.

"These things aren't any worse than sardines," said Alex, as she grabbed her own herring and started to eat.

"And you don't see me eating those either do you?" replied Becky. Anyways if you excuse me, sergeant I think I'll take your advice and get one of those flyboys onto the dance floor.

"Hold on Private, have a herring first," ordered Alex.

"Ah but Serge," whined the dark-haired prairie girl.

"You will not insult our hosts, especially when it is given to us as an honour," said Alex.

Becky sighed, she hated when the Sergeant was right. She glanced over at the very slim Rivka and imagined just how skinny she must have been two years ago, when the Canadian Army had to liberate the country. Having rebelled against the German occupation Holland had nearly been starved to death in retaliation. The situation had been so dire that the Canadians had not only open negotiations with the Germans for a temporary cease fire to stave off millions dying but the German Heer command had agreed. It had been a close thing but the Canadians had managed to pull off a minor miracle and much of the population had been saved.

It was the common opinion within the Army that the Krauts had agreed so that the Canadians and their allies would expend time and massive resources trying to save civilians without any value to the war effort, and would have to continue to expend resources keeping them alive. They may have been right, but the Canadians didn't give a shit. Not to save millions of people that could be saved right next to you would have made them too much like the Germans.

So, with reluctance (not to mention the rest of her pint of beer) Becky ate a raw herring and smiled, while she did it.

After she finished, Becky had every intention of going to deal with those American airmen. However, just as she was heading off Rivka came back to the table again. Only this time she was carrying a tray with four shot glasses full of jenever, a Dutch flavoured light whiskey that was the only hard liquor that the tavern sold.

"Rivka, I think the beers and the food were enough congratulations, we can't accept a round of shots as well," explained Alex to the waitress.

"No, no this is not from my vather, this is from the women at that table," said Rivka pointing to one of the booths.

Becky was already looking in that general direction so she glanced over and said "Okay, who are they?"

They were behind Alex so the young sergeant was the last to see who it was. When she did Alex inwardly groaned. "That's Leftenant Johnson, our new commanding officer, and her walker's crew," she said outwardly to her own crew.

As Alex was talking, the other four young women had gotten up and moved towards where the other walker crew was sitting. All of them also bore shot glasses.

"Sergeant, I was hoping you'd share a toast with me and my ladies," said Lieutenant Johnson.

Alex appreciated the gesture; the Lieutenant was trying to make amends. Lord knew the army was hard enough for women, the last thing they needed right now was for them to be at each other backs.

"Alright Leftenant Johnson, but what should we drink to?" she asked the dark-haired officer. Alex was interested in hearing what Lieutenant Johnson would say and thereby get a better measure of the woman.

Chantal answered the question before the British aristocratic officer could reply. "We drink to the men in our lives of course," she said, being Acadian the last person she wanted to drink to was the British King which had been the obvious choice.

Her response caused confused looks among the British walker crew, until Alex said, "My driver is talking about our walkers, Ma'am. It's sort of a running joke among female walker personnel. We refer to them as 'he' and joke about they're the only real men you can completely trust in this man's army."

"That's a bit cynical isn't it sergeant?" replied Lieutenant Johnson.

"Let's see how cynical she thinks it is after her first shower," mutter Sarah who after she said it, and realized she'd spoken aloud, added a hasty "Ma'am."

To her credit Lieutenant Johnson didn't respond to Sarah's comment instead she said "regardless toasting our walkers sounds like an excellent idea: here's to Sting."

"And here's to Winnie," said Alex with equal relish.

All eight women raised their shot glasses and downed the jenever.

After they'd downed the shots, Lieutenant Johnson turned to a corporal on her crew and said "I believe I heard one of Winne's crew plans to engage those American Airmen Corporal Cox. Why don't you and the rest of the crew assist her in that effort?"

Corporal Cox, who looked to be in her late twenties, which made her by far the oldest woman there, replied "Are you sure Ma'am?"

"Yes, quite sure corporal," was the officer's reply.

Alex recognized what was going to happen next and was willing to help out. Turning to Sarah and Chantal she said, "You two help Becky dance those airmen's feet off," Her tone though still polite, had the air of an order which the other too women rose to obey.

In a flash, just the Lieutenant and the Sergeant were left at the table.

Alex sat back and sipped her beer, letting the tension build. She was a woman who was comfortable with silence and more than willing to let the other woman stew.

"Sergeant I feel that there are a few things that we need to clear up between us," Lieutenant Johnson said as she finally sat down.

"Ma'am?" asked Alex.

"First off, I am sorry that my presence has wrecked your chance for promotion. However, what's done is done and I am in command of the walker platoon now and I expect the support of my platoon sergeant; of you, when I give my orders," said the Lieutenant in a gush of words.

Alex couldn't help it, but the obvious anxiety of the Lieutenant's speech made her smile, "You practice that speech for a long time Ma'am," she said to the officer.

"For most of the afternoon," replied the officer with some obvious relief. "Listen, I know I'm green as hell, but I know enough about being an officer to know that I need your support if we're going to succeed in our missions, and keep everyone alive," said Lieutenant Johnson. This time the flow of words was at a more normal pace; though they also had an air of earnestness to them.

"Alright Leftenant I'll have your back; are you willing to listen to my first piece of advice?" asked Alex.

The dark curly haired woman just nodded.

Alex took this time to take another small sip of her beer. Despite just knocking back a shot of hard liquor, Alex wasn't a heavy drinker and she would nurse this pint for the rest of the night. Putting down the beer, she said "Your job is making sure the battalion succeeds in its mission. My job is making sure that everyone has the highest chance of surviving that is possible. Do not confuse the two. As well, keep in mind that we both can do our job perfectly and our people are still going to die. That's the nature of war; of life. Forget that and you'll shatter and make it that much harder for the rest of us. Remember a lot of people in this battalion, hell this army are just itching to see us fail, if a man cries over a fallen buddy, it's no big thing, losing a friend is tough. You shed a tear; and it's proof that all women are too emotional to stand up to the stresses of combat," Alex's eyes turned hard, and she said "Do you understand this?"

"I've never heard it put in such stark terms before but yes I understand," replied the British officer.

The silence started to build once again as the two women quietly sipped their drinks. Finally, Johnson broke the silence and asked, "Are the stories true?"

"Which stories Ma'am?" Alex genuinely didn't know which stories the Lieutenant was talking about. And if you have done more than one thing which people are telling stories about that probably isn't a good thing.

"About how you single handedly created the situation that forced your Army into letting women fight," replied the young officer.

Alex chuckled and then said "Oh that. I was there, and maybe I got the puck out of our end, but it was Leftenant Grassa who put it into the net."

When she saw that Lieutenant Johnson wasn't satisfied with that response, Alex knew that she wasn't going to get away without telling the full story. So, after taking another sip from her beer, Alex started in.

"It was last summer, Leftenant Grassa was in charge of the maintenance and repair platoon that I had been assigned to. We were part of 2$^{nd}$ Brigade's HQ and we'd been working on repairing a number of vehicles all day. It was late, well past midnight, but we'd managed to get everything at least working ahead of the other maintenance platoons. We were just cleaning up and grabbing a mug of composite tea when the alarms for a terror raid started up. We were near the HQ and even with our limited lighting we stuck out in the night. So, we knew we were going to be a target.

"This had happened before, of course, but this time... We'd just put in all those hours getting these machines back together and here Jerry was, going to mash it all back to hell. Right then, I was too tired to be scared, instead I was pissed off. So instead of heading to a shelter and away from the fight, I did what any good soldier did; I headed towards the guns. We'd been working on some walkers that night and I knew they were ready to go. We also had ammunition on hand for test firing the machine guns to make sure the mechanisms worked, and gas in jerry cans to top off fuel tanks. So, I grabbed a box of 50 cal. and a near full jerry can and started to lug both towards one of the open Guardians.

"I was about half way there when I felt someone else take up the weight of the Jerry can and then I saw the rest of the platoon running past me heading towards the walkers. The Lieutenant then slid up next to me and said, 'Sergeant if you're going to do something truly stupid could you let me know first; you still need my permission.'

"I was too dumd struck to do anything but grin and speed up to a run," Alex then paused and took a full swallow of her beer.

"And then what happened?" asked Lieutenant Johnson, her attention still fixed upon the red-haired non-com.

"Pretty much what's in the reports. We armed up and got moving and got to the Brigade HQ just in time to sae a whole lot of brass from being killed. We saved their butts, including the Divisional Commander, who was there on an inspection. When he got over the shock of still being alive, he asked what we wanted as a reward for going above and beyond. It was the Leftenant who said we wanted the option to serve in combat," finished Alex.

"And what was the general's response?"

"He laughed and said he would take it 'under advisement'. I doubt it would have gone anywhere, if it hadn't of been for a CBC reporter, who ass we also saved. He thought that our idea had merit and made the story too large for the Army to ignore," Alex said with a grimace, as if she was embarrassed about having to rely on the press to get what she wanted.

"Is that what you discuss in your 'talk'?" The British woman asked changing course

Alex raised an eyebrow, and said, "Oh you've heard about it have you?" Every time a new walker crewman came into the platoon Alex gave them an orientation lecture, and explained what her expectations were and the realities of being a woman in combat. That this was strictly a woman only lecture and no one talked about it afterwards, had given the lecture a bit of mystique within the battalion; that according to Becky, 'gossiped more than a bunch of spinsters making a crazy quilt'.

"Leftenant Colonel Goodbar told me about it. He said that you were going to give it to all of the British women that were joining the platoon. He also said that if I was really as smart as what I appeared to be, that I would take off my epaulettes and attend as well," said Lieutenant Johnson with a genuine smile.

Alex smiled as well. She then gave her beer another sip. "I've heard worst ideas," she said finally.

# Chapter Four: The Talk

Major William Steves knew that a lot of brass was watching the Seaforths right now with all these 'special projects' going on. If he wanted any future in this man's army then he wasn't going to have any choice but to give the 'special handling' that the rest of the command gave to the girl walker crews and mechanics. So when Sergeant Mackenzie made the usual completely unreasonable request to use one of the lecture halls for briefing the British girls he surprised the young non-com by signing off on the request without his usual inquiries making sure that it was really needed.

Though he would never tell anyone, the truth was that he was scared of the red headed Sergeant. Lieutenant Grassa had been a pushy bitch but he could intimidate her when necessary. Mackenzie on the other hand, despite being the smallest woman in the platoon, just didn't scare. He'd tried, and he'd seen others also try, and the Sergeant had just looked at them with those hard-grey eyes of hers that just dared you to bring your worst. According to battalion legend, when she was just a mechanic, a couple of male privates had caught her in an alleyway and brought their worst. Mackenzie had spent two weeks in the stockade for fighting. The two privates ended up being medically discharged.

Pushing those unpleasant thoughts aside, Major Steves went back to signing orders and filling forms that someone else thought were important.

**

When Alex and Ida entered the lecture room, they were greeted by ten or so British Faces of the new Walker crews and their maintenance personnel. On the one hand the sergeant felt grateful for the additional manpower but their number effectively doubled the platoon's size which in turn meant a lot more paperwork, even if she was back to being Platoon Sergeant.

Among the waiting faces, three stood out. One was of course Lieutenant Johnson herself, sans her officer epaulettes. The other Alex recognized as one of Blastfield's aides; one of his male aides. The last person that stood out to Alex was a young woman dressed in a mixture of civilian and military dress that marked her as one of the most quixotic of adversaries for the army: a reporter.

"Oh, this is going to be interesting," said Ida to her shorter superior.

Alex didn't say a word. Instead she squared her shoulders and marched brusquely up to the male lieutenant. Giving him a sharp salute, she then said "Sir this orientation is for women only."

The British officer returned the salute with a lazy, indifferent one himself then said, "the Brigadier has assigned me as the platoon's neutral observer. It is important that I observe all lectures and briefings of a military matter."

"Ah, then you are not required to be here then sir, as this lecture is strictly around the issues of female hygiene within the modern combat environment. Due to its importance, it has to be a rather graphic and detailed lecture," said Alex with an almost apologetic tone.

The lieutenant blanched as he realized what exactly Alex was talking about. With a barely audible, "yes yes quite right." He retreated out of the room as fast as his staff legs could carry him.

There was an audible sigh of relief in the room as the door closed behind the staff officer. Turning back to Lieutenant Johnson, Alex was gratified to see a silently mouthed 'thank you' from the dark-haired woman.

The small Sergeant then turned her attention to the female reporter. With no military etiquette whatsoever, Alex marched up to the reporter and said, "You're leaving too."

Alex's voice was cold and her eyes took on a glassy shine. The temperature dropped several degrees as the mood in the room went from lighthearted and jovial to serious as everyone realized that violence was just moments away.

The reporter looked shocked by Alex's statement and the very real danger she felt herself in. Deciding that discretion was the better part of valor, the reporter gathered up her things and quietly followed the male officer out of the room.

As she went by, Ida whispered "smart choice" to the reporter. From experience Ida knew that despite her size Alex Mackenzie was one of the most dangerous people in the battalion. She had absolutely no qualms about using violence, nor about killing for that matter. In confrontations with drunken soldiers or rampaging zombies Alex never backed down and wasn't afraid to be messy when she had to be. That she backed up that attitude with the savage skills that modern warfare had taught her; made Alex a dangerous person whether in a walker or not.

Once the reporter left the room, Alex turned to the rest of the women and said "Right, now that the distractions have been removed, I expect to have your full attention. And as my old mechanics instructor used to say 'the only dumb question is the one not asked' if you have a question, I will take them at the end of the lecture. If you can't remember what the question was by then, it must not have been very important in the first place. Clear!"

"Yes Sergeant!" replied the entire room as one.

Alex just nodded, and then started into her standard orientation speech that Ida had heard many times before.

"Welcome to the Seaforth Highlanders of Canada. You are joining the best battalion of the best brigade of the best division of the best army that the allies have. The Seaforths have seen near continuous combat since 1943 and we have the scars and bragging right that comes with that level of fighting. The walker platoon might be the newest part of the battalion and we might not always be welcome by other members of the unit, but you will give it the respect that it deserves. Clear?"

"Yes Sergeant!" was the reply.

"Good. Now unlike our allies, the Canadian Army has dispersed its walkers among its infantry battalions as part of its support company, along with its anti-tank guns, mortars, Bren carriers and pioneers. This has allowed the walkers to train with the infantry and the Alfreds to become an effective fighting whole. As a result, we're able to accomplish the same combat mission as an American or British battalion but with three quarters of the personnel," continued Alex.

Watching from the sidelines Ida noted some disbelief on the British faces. It didn't surprise her, since the First World War, Canadians have been showing the 'senior force' how to fight smarter, not just harder; often to little effect and even less credit.

Alex ploughed on, "By now I'm sure you've all experienced at least one of Jerry's terror raids. If not then you soon will, because it is the favorite tactical engagement for him in the Canadian sector. From brutal experience we have learned that walkers are best equipped to counter these terror attacks. As a result, standard operating procedure for a Battalion in the rear area is to have half of its walker platoon on standby during the night ready to respond to a raid. The other half is to be kept combat ready and expected to follow the active half of the platoon into combat as quickly as humanly possible. If the original crew is not available in a timely manner then maintenance personnel will take their place. Clear!"

"Yes Sergeant," said the rest of the room.

"Now such a high tempo of readiness combined with the fact that during an attack we're on the bleeding edge will lead to a lot of pressure upon all personnel. Try to be as supportive of each other as possible. Now is not the time to undercut each other, especially in front of any male personnel. They already think that we don't belong here, don't give them additional dirt to bury us with.

"Further regarding men; best not to trust any of them. Now I assume that all of you have received your contraception shots before being sent to the front?" Alex asked.

When she saw all the nods Alex said "Good. Now I assume they're still pushing that bullshit about protecting you from pregnancy in case you're captured? Well the truth is that you have a lot more to fear from Canadian dicks than German. That is why you will never go anywhere on base by yourself. Always move in groups of two or more. This is especially the case with going to the latrine, the showers, or anywhere else where you may be caught in a vulnerable position. As well, as part of your kit you will be issued with a set of Canadian Women's Mark 1 brass knuckles," said Alex as she held up her own set.

With a nod from Alex, Ida started to hand out the knuckles to all the women in the room.

"You will keep them within arm's reach at all times, and you will not hesitate to use them on any man who appears to be having ill intentions towards you; no matter the rank. I want to really stress this. If you feel that the division commander himself is not taking the hints. Use his balls as a punching bag with these and report the incident to me or the Leftenant right away. If we can get ahead of the story, we can hopefully keep you out of the stockade," said Alex

Ida looked over towards the new Lieutenant whose eyes were wide and her complexion had turned a Zombie's white. Obviously, she hadn't known that she'd be volunteered as part of Alex's 'punch the Division Commander and we'll try and get you out of it' promise. But to her credit she didn't contradict Alex and just let her continue.

"By the way, the chances of the male soldier getting changed are next to zero. So, don't expect 'official channels' to protect you. However, at least in this battalion it's well known that all women carry these knuckles and that we're not afraid to use them. So, we've largely got the problem licked in house. However, others are not aware so be careful.

Ida noticed that Alex made no comment about the other reason why women inside of the unit generally didn't have to worry about the rest of the battalion and that was Alex herself. Like a lot of other Sergeants Alex was more than willing to use back of the barrack discipline and that if she tangled with a man that had threatened one of her girls, they'd be found later alive but temporarily combat ineffective. The other Sergeants were well aware of this and came down hard on their own men because they knew if they didn't Alex would.

Ida didn't know how the other battalions handled these issues, only that things hadn't gotten out of hand in the Seaforths and that couldn't be said about the army as a whole.

"Alright now that we've dealt with the problems unique to women in combat, lets deal with some other issues," said Alex as she pulled out a tanker's helmet from her rucksack.

"This is the current issue helmet for all tank and walker crews. While you are in this platoon, when you are in your walker, you will wear your issued helmet at all times. I know the tankers and quite a few walker crews like their more stylish berets. However, there are good reasons to wear a helmet. Sergeant," said Alex as she gestured to Ida.

Ida then pulled out her own helmet. It had obviously seen some use, being dented and nicked in over a dozen places.

"How many combat missions has that helmet seen?" asked Alex.

"Two Sergeant," replied Ida.

There was an audible gasp from the room.

"You'd be surprised how motivating people trying to kill you is when it comes to how hard you'll maneuver your walker. Keep that in mind next time you to want complain about helmet hair," Alex said.

Her role in the lecture complete, Ida watched Alex go onto other matters and then answer a dozen inane questions at the end of the lecture. Looking over the new members of the platoon she was glad to see that the new Lieutenant had taken a lot of what Alex was saying to heart. This bode well as far as Ida was concerned. Any officer who was willing to learn was okay in Ida's book.

# Chapter Five: Preparation

With the breaking-in of a new officer and the initial talk to new recruits over and done with, all that was left was fighting and winning the war. The wiser heads at 21st Army Group decided that it was time for the Canadians to get back onto the offensive.

For the past two years, the Allies had tried to breach the German Rhine defense to the South without much success. Finally, someone at SHAFE had looked at a map and realized that the entire Canadian 1st Army was actually north of the Rhine and maybe it might be a good idea to try attacking there for once.

Or at least that's how many officers with the 1st Canadian Army felt as they found out that it was going to be their sector that was going to kick off the Spring offensive of 1947. The overall offensive would be of two parts. The 1st Canadian Corps with the three Canadian Infantry Divisions and the two independent Armoured Brigades would punch through the deeply layered German defences along the Dutch border creating a corridor that the 2nd Canadian Corps, which had the two Canadian Armoured Divisions, would then use to breakthrough to the North German Plain and onto Osnabruck. The Dutch Corps with two Dutch Infantry Divisions and what remained of the 1st Polish Armoured Division would be held in reserve to either check a German counter attack too strong for the Canadians or to keep the corridor between the Canadian lines and Osnabruck open. The entire U.S. 9th Army was ready to swing north and push on to Hamburg if the Canadians succeeded in their attacks.

It was a bold plan; one that depended upon skill, daring, and more than a little bit of luck to break the Canadians' way. Fortunately, the Seaforths only had to worry about punching through the second German defensive belt, which was a big enough job as far as Lieutenant Colonel Goodbar was concerned. Set about a thousand metres behind the first line of defences, the second line had been reinforced by an old German favorite: the Pantherturm. These forts consisted of a Panther turret emplaced in a concrete bunker on a natural or manmade rise. Surrounding this main bunker were secondary bunkers equipped with mortars, 50 and 75mm anti-tank guns, and 20mm anti-aircraft guns. Not to mention more machine guns than had a right to exist. And these were only the defences that intelligence could identify. It really bothered Goodbar that no Rift Tech defences been identified. Division intelligence believed that this indicated that the Germans hadn't used their Rift Tech weapon systems in the defence on this sector. The Lieutenant Colonel didn't believe that for a second.

"Well hopefully we will be hitting them hard enough and fast enough that it won't matter," Goodbar said to his planning staff.

"Sir," asked one of his staffers.

"Oh, I was just wondering how the Germans are going to use their Rift Tech to screw us?" he said loud enough for everyone to hear.

"Division, Corps and Army Intel all believe that they've not deployed anything in the areas other than their terror units. And these units are unsuited for defences in depth," said his intelligence officer confidently.

"Does that sound like the Germans we know?" replied Goodbar

"Their resources are already stretched; would they use their limited rift tech as part of their static defences that might never be used?" asked another staff officer.

Goodbar sighed and then said "You all are probably right, but I just can't believe that we would be that lucky."

All of the Seaforth's staff looked back and forth at each other. Their commanding officer had a point. When attacking the Germans, planning for the worst and then getting it was pretty much standing operating procedure.

Major Masse, the Seaforth's second in Command cleared his throat and then said "I'll contact the division artillery commander directly. Maybe we can get some of their Turing artillery engines available for fast calculations if were hit by unexpected German counterattacks.

Goodbar looked up from the maps and said, "Good idea, also make sure we have a direct link to both Grizzly walkers. Any response we potentially use is guaranteed to be centred around the walker platoon.

A junior staff officer muttered something that Goodbar missed. "What was that Dalton?" he asked, putting the young lieutenant on the spot.

"I was just thanking god that Sergeant Mackenzie is their sir," replied Dalton, embarrassed for saying the phrase aloud.

"I believe the British Leftentant will handle herself adequately Leftentant but I agree I feel better knowing that Winnie and her crew are there as well."

\*\*

Right then Winnie and the rest of the walker Platoon were working with the Seaforth's infantry companies in preparation for their attack. One of the walker's most important jobs early in the attack was to help the pioneer platoon and the divisional engineers clear a path through the dragon teeth. From experiments that the Americans had done: a Grizzly walker fist could level an individual tooth with two or three hits. A Jackson or Guardian light walker could do the same with half a dozen strikes. The result was still a pretty rough path but tanks and Kangaroos could cross; which was the important thing.

However, the most important job for the walkers in the assault was the neutralization of the various pillboxes and other German defences along the line. Here the Guardians were actually more important than the Grizzly's. For years it had been shown that the best way to break a German's hold on a pillbox was with flame. This was why the Canadians helped develop and improve on the WASP, and why even in 1947 there were never enough Churchill Crocodile, flame throwing tanks to meet demand.

The Guardians with their tempest flamethrowers helped fill that need. And in this case were a better choice because they could move through the dragon's teeth and get to support the infantry directly. Winnie's and the other Grizzlies' job in these situations were to not only keep the German's heads down but to also draw fire away from the lighter walkers as they closed. This was not an easy job, and required a skilled crew to pull off and survive. Winnie's crew was up to the task, it remained to be seen how well Lieutenant Johnson and the crew of Sting could handle it.

From Alex's perspective the answer appeared to be a cautious yes. Lieutenant Johnson seemed capable of making quick decisions and while she and her crew made mistakes; it was never the same mistake twice. What it really came down to was could they get good at doing Lats. This was hockey slang for stepping sideways on skates. The slang arose because in both cases it was a rather hard maneuver to pull off, in the case of the walker it required the coordination between the driver (who couldn't see sideways) and the commander (who had to stick her head out of the walker and give her directions). The advantage of the maneuver was that it could throw the enemies aim completely off which allowed a walker enough time to get its own shot off against the target.

Chantal and Alex had been working with Private Campbell, Sting's driver, for the past two days getting her used to the feel of the maneuver. She'd gotten the gist of it, but whether she could do it while under fire was something yet to be seen.

During one of the breaks, Alex indulged herself with one of the Coca Colas that she had left and a quiet moment to herself. That was until Lieutenant Johnson came over.

"Ma'am?" Alex said as she started to get up from where she was sitting.

"Oh, please stay where you are. May I join you?" Johnson asked Alex.

What she really wanted was for the officer to leave her alone and let her finish her Coke in peace, but of course pointed to the ground beside her and said, "Of course Ma'am."

Her Lieutenant sat down with what smelled like a mug of real coffee. For a couple of minutes, the two young women just sat there alone in their thoughts; then finally the young officer broke her silence.

"Sergeant I'd like to thank you not only for all your hard work, but the support you…," Lieutenant Johnson started to say.

"Ma'am I'm just doing my job as the Platoon Sergeant that's all," interrupted Alex before things got awkward.

"Well thank you for that," said her commanding officer who waited several seconds for continuing, "But I have a few non-military questions that I'd like to ask you."

Alex had an idea of what the questions might be and said, "Shoot, I'll try and answer them as best as I can."

"How are you handling Miss Warren's attention?" the Lieutenant asked with a certain degree of delight.

"Better me than you?" asked Alex with a wry smile.

Since the Sergeant had banished the reporter from the women's briefing, Anne Marie Warren had become obsessed with Sergeant Mackenzie. She had wanted to know everything about her, trying to figure out how someone so small could project such a lethal bearing.

"It does appear that you are the bone that she refuses to let go of," Lieutenant Johnson observed.

"She's been trying to get a story from one of Winnie's crew or the maintenance staff but so far she's been stonewalled. I'm afraid the she may just get frustrated and make up the story herself," replied Alex.

"You have a very cynical view of the press, Sergeant," said the Lieutenant.

"It's well-earned," said Alex with a note of finality.

Sensing that was the end of that topic, Lieutenant Johnson changed tacks. "Major Steves."

"He's a prick isn't he," Alex said, cutting off her superior officer before she could find a longer more polite way of saying the same thing.

"Yes, and completely blind to competence when it is right in front of him," the Lieutenant said.

"He's the worst officer in the battalion who's been promoted to a position where he can do the least amount of damage. Fortunately, Leftenant Colonel Goodbar directly attaches the control of the walker platoon to the battalion HQ so you don't have to worry about Steves fucking up when it really matters.

Alex's reply caused the Lieutenant to frown then she said "The language of both the Canadian men and women,"

"It's more blue than what you're used to?" Alex asked, guessing the problem.

"Yes," I've been around British soldiers and I'm not a prude, but. Is this a Seaforth thing?" she asked earnestly.

Alex just laughed and said, "If you talk to the men who were here before the walker platoons joined the battalion, they'll tell you that the language had improved quite a bit."

Lieutenant Johnson's cheeks reddened a bit as she said "Oh dear."

"Anyways, from what I understand the Canadian soldier including the officers have always been described as a bit rougher than their English counterparts. I not really sure why," explained Alex.

"Does that include the Canadian female soldiers," Lieutenant Johnson asked, with a ghost of smile.

"In general, yes, I believe so, though I can't recall Private May ever swearing since I've known her. So, mileage may vary," Alex replied.

"She does seem to be the most 'girly' member of the platoon I've met so far. My gunner tells me that she positively gushed about our Grizzly's name, and wouldn't stop talking about it till she found out how he got his name," the dark-haired officer replied.

The comment made Alex visibly wince. "Tell your gunner that when it comes to her doing her job, she should treat what Sarah says as gospel, in regards to everything else… Well she's obsessed with this children's book by some British professor, Token or something. She gets a little bent out of shape when she thinks she may have found someone who shares her obsession," she said apologetically.

"It's Professor Tolkien and The Hobbit is a perfectly reasonable book to get obsess about. On the surface it may appear to be a simple children's story but it also talks about personal responsibility and how to stay true to yourself in the most onerous of circumstances. Something I need reminding of in my present employment," Lieutenant Johnson said overly primly.

Alex was about to say something but thought the better of it and just said "Yes Ma'am."

# amazon.com

SUHfoodmlo

**Your order of June 9, 2020 (Order ID 111-0523354-8350626)**

| Qty. | Item | Item Price | Total |
|---|---|---|---|
| 10 | **Seaforth's Ladies: Revised** Addison, Sandy Edward --- Paperback B08PLYN3WW B08PLYN3WW 9798645201920 | $2.15 | $21.50 |

This shipment completes your order.

| | |
|---|---|
| Subtotal | $21.50 |
| Shipping & Handling | $20.99 |
| Order Total | $42.49 |
| Paid via credit/debit | $42.49 |

**Return or replace your item**
Visit Amazon.com/returns

7/UHfoodmlo/-10 of 10-//UPS-EAST-NEXT/std-int-us-
ca/315608I6/0721-15:30/0720-19:03

A1

# Chapter Six: Zero Hour

All too quickly the day of the attack arrived, and the walker platoon of the Seaforth Highlanders of Canada found itself waiting for the attack with the rest of 2nd Canadian Brigade. 1st Canadian Brigade started the attack on the first line of defences in the 1st Canadian Infantry Division's sector. All along the line the sharp report of the 25prds was mixed with the deeper and louder crump of the 5.5-inch guns. It was an impressive amount of noise but the veterans of the division knew that while the Germans in the fortifications may be shaken, it was still going to take infantry to dig the enemy out of their positions.

Finally, it was time, 1st Canadian Brigade had done a good enough job of breaching the first line of defences that the 2nd could start moving. As one, dozens of Kangaroo armoured personnel carriers started their engines. The Seaforths and other battalions were going into the fight with every advantage that high command could give them. Along with enough APCs to move the entire Brigade, the 2nd Canadian Brigade was joined in the attack by the tanks of the Fort Gerry Horse Regiment, and as many Churchill Crocodiles as the 79th Armoured Division was willing to part with. 1st Canadian Division command had requested a number of Petard AVREs hoping that they could help blast a path through the dragon's teeth, instead they got a bunch of Churchills modified with Rift Tech. Called Meteors, these Churchills were equipped with a large bank of rockets which contained 'metal weakening' enzymes that would melt the steel the Germans were using in their bunkers. While the division planning staff was fine with this substitution, Alex was more cynical. Other than walkers and particular Winnie, Alex found the claims of what Rift Tech could do rarely matched the actual battlefield performance. Personally, she would have preferred using the version of the Churchill that made a really loud bang, but those decisions were beyond her pay grade.

As they moved through the 1st Canadian Brigade's area of attack even the veterans like her were starting to become cautiously optimistic. Large holes had been blasted and cut through the mind fields, wire and dragon's teeth. German bunkers had been blasted open and rendered useless. The price had still been high however. Everywhere were the mangled remains of Canadian vehicles and Alfred bodies. Not to mention the large number of Kangaroos heading back to Canadian lines piled high with the wounded. Still there were enough of 1st Canadian Brigade's infantry and Alfreds to hold the positions they'd taken.

Winnie and the other members of the Seaforth's walker platoon, were with the leading edge of the attack. So, they got a front roll seat as the artillery shifted targets and started hitting the German's second belt of defences. The artillery was hitting the objectives for half an hour before the battalion headquarters came over the horn. They wanted to talk to the Lieutenant but Alex listened in regardless.

"Echo to Echo7Alpha, are the walkers ready to move?" It was Lieutenant Colonel Goodbar himself asking the question. Alex knew that she really shouldn't be eavesdropping on the conversation but she figured that the Lieutenant would forgive her.

"Echo7Alpha to Echo, were ready as we'll ever be," replied Lieutenant Johnson.

"Good. We're about to get the go order, follow your training, and in the heat of the moment, remember even a bad choice is better than no choice. Also, if you got the time, ask Sergeant Mackenzie what she would do," he said. It might have seen strange for a Lieutenant Colonel to talk to a Lieutenant directly; but the walkers were the most concentrated source of fire within the battalion and Goodbar liked to control them through his HQ.

"I was going to do that regardless, but I sure she appreciated hearing that suggestion from you," Johnson said.

The Seaforth's CO laughed and said, "Yeah she's probably listening isn't she."

"She'd be dumb not to," replied the Lieutenant.

Alex felt somewhat vindicated by the answer.

"Keep her alive, and she'll do the same for you, Leftenant Johnson," was the CO's last piece of advice.

A minute later the artillery barrage started to lighten and Alex saw the yellow flare, the signal to start the attack, while over the net a sharp whistle could be heard.

"Alright Chantal move toward the dragon's teeth," said Alex as she popped the hatch and took her usual command position behind the M2 Browning.

Moving forward, Winnie was joined not only by the other walkers, but also by the Kangaroos carrying the assault companies. The tanks would hold back until clear paths through the Dragon Teeth were made, offering direct fire support where they could.

As they closed with the German defences, Alex saw that the artillery bombardment started to include more smoke shells, offering cover to the assault units. "Hopefully the Germans hadn't found a way to see through smoke or we're fucked," Alex said to herself.

Getting to the Dragon's Teeth; the young sergeant saw that there were several holes blasted in the works, but there was no continuous path that would allow the armour to pass through. She also heard the ping of shrapnel ricocheting off of Winnie as the German mortars started to rain bombs upon where the walker now stood.

"Chantal lateral left, we're in a pre-plotted zone for their mortars," Alex ordered as she sunk down behind the hatch.

"Second and Third Sections get to breaking teeth. Winnie we're on overwatch. Smoke then blast anything that even looks like it's about to shoot," Lieutenant Johnson ordered her over the platoon radio channel.

"Yes Ma'am," everyone said in reply.

As the women started their work, the Kangaroos that were carrying the lead company were maneuvering to allow the infantry to get out as safely as possible. The Alfreds were the first out of their transports, their heads turning methodically from left to right looking for targets. One of the mechanical men went down as a mortar bomb exploded right at its feet. Others were staggered as German machine guns started to open up on the robotic infantry. But in complete silence the Alfreds brought up their own machine guns, and answered the German fire with their own short very controlled burst.

"Gunner; target one hundred metres, ten degrees from centre left and five degrees positive. Fire WP followed up by HE," Alex ordered seeing the flash of one of the machine guns.

Quickly Sarah maneuvered the 75mm cannon into position and as soon the machine gun fired another burst, she made some fine adjustments and pulled the trigger. All sound was drowned out inside the walker as the main gun fired sending the white phosphorous shell towards the German position. The empty shell casing clanked onto Winnie's floor and Becky rammed home a fresh high explosive shell into the cannon. She patted Sarah on the shoulder letting the gunner know she was clear and the cannon roared again.

Because Alex hadn't ordered what she had wanted for the third round, Sarah took it upon herself to choose. "Load WP," she shouted towards Becky.

"WP aye," Becky said, confirming the choice. She then loaded the round and once again tapped Sarah to let her know she was clear.

From the command hatch Alex had her hands full looking for targets, watching for hazards to avoid and keeping from being slammed too hard into the hatch as Chantal maneuvered Winnie around to prevent him from becoming too easy of a target.

"Chantal advance through the Dragon's Teeth, we need to keep moving forward. The pathway to your left looks clear," she ordered.

As Chantel complied Alex hoped that the German doctrine regarding where vehicle landmines should be placed, hadn't yet caught up with battlefield reality. While the Germans had laced, the Dragon's Teeth with anti-personnel mines, in the past they hadn't added any anti-vehicle mines to the mix to take out walkers that move through the obstacles. So far, their luck had held.

WHAM!

He whole walker shook and as it took a hit from something.

"Call out," Alex shrieked into the intercom as she crouched down into the walker crew compartment.

"Good," said Chantal

"Fine," said Sarah

"Shit," said Becky being more truthful than the others.

"Echo7Beta, this is Echo7Alpha; status?" Lieutenant Johnson called out over the radio.

"Were fine Echo7Alpha, no penetration," Alex replied.

"Good. We got the bastards that shot you, so back to work," the Lieutenant ordered.

"Ma'am. Thank you, Ma'am," replied Alex, as she rose back up through in the command hatch. Only then did she see the large gouge taken out of Winnie's right shoulder plate above the arm. Six inches lower and it would have taken off the entire arm. She tried not to think too long on the fact that if the round had been two feet to the left, she'd be dead.

'Shit we just used up our luck for the day,' Alex thought to herself as she re-manned the Browning, and started to once again look for new targets.

Wind caused the artillery smoke to clear for a second, and Alex saw an important one.

"Gunner, Pantherturm ten degrees right and twenty degrees up. Fire whatever is in the tube followed by WP. We need to keep that thing blind," Alex said and she lined the turret up in her fifty calibre sights.

As she depressed the trigger, the weapon's half inch rounds started to spit out, sparking off the Panther turret. She knew that she wasn't doing any damage but the tracer would make it easier for Sarah to spot the target.

Alex had let off maybe twenty rounds when it became clear that she wasn't the only one who had noticed the Pantherturm. Several rockets came out of nowhere to strike the turret. The explosions that the rockets made were nothing like what Alex had seen before. They were obviously shaped charges, but they seemed to cause the turret's metal to spray up when they hit. Even stranger, the fifty calibre rounds she was still firing were no longer sparking off the turret but actually penetrating.

Then the turret exploded; with such a powerful blast that it just disappeared. The only evidence of its existence were the gobs of thick metallic sludge that landed near Winnie.

"Okay maybe there is something to the eggheads' enzyme weapons after all," Alex said aloud.

"Uhmm Ma'am. There isn't a target there anymore," Sarah said over the intercom her own voice betraying her own amazement.

"Agreed, I'll find something else for you to shoot at soon, don't worry," replied Alex.

"Jeez, where can we get some of those rockets," asked Ida over the platoon channel.

"Cut the chatter people," ordered Lieutenant Johnson before Alex could do the same.

Looking around to get a better feel for the battle, it appeared to Alex that things were going reasonably well. Two paths large enough for tanks and APCs had been opened though the dragon teeth. The assault companies were busy taking over the initial defensive line and the follow up companies were moving forward. The Fort Gerry tanks having moved through the Dragon's teeth were spreading out and adding their own fire, decreasing the number of possible targets. Casualties were being taken but nowhere near what the cynics (like Alex) had feared.

It was then that the Germans launched their counter attack.

"Zombies, hundreds of them!" said a frantic voice over the battalion net.

Alex frantically looked to see where the attack was coming from, but she couldn't see them anywhere.

"Behind us, they're attacking the flanks!" shouted Ida over the platoon's channel.

"Thors! Thors to our front," said another voice over the net.

Alex swung around, to look behind her, let the tanks deal with the Thors for now. From Winnie's high position, she saw what the Germans had done. In the area between the first line of defences and the second row of Dragon's teeth they had dug large pits and stacked unactivated zombies in their hundreds. Then covering them with camouflaged grates they had waited until a time of their choosing to activate them.

Seeing the zombies moving rapidly towards their support columns, Alex was galvanized into action. Scrambling out of the walker, she swung the Browning around to face the rear. Then with a foot braced on either side of the 75mm she opened up on a group of zombies nearest to the walker.

Once again, the half inch rounds sped out toward a target. This time they tore through dead flesh, taking the German reanimated troopers apart and making sure they stayed dead this time.

Suddenly the Browning ran dry. "Becky bring up another box of 50 cal," Alex ordered over the intercom.

When Winnies loader/radio operator didn't appear with a fresh box of ammunition, Alex shouted the order again. It was only then that the sergeant realized that when she had leapt out of the command hatch her plugs for her headset had disconnected! Hoping to get her crewmates attention, Alex stamped hard on Winnies metal hull.

Within seconds Becky emerged from Winnies with a fresh box of ammunition in one hand.

As she reloaded the 50 cal she shouted at Alex "Message from the Leftenant. She said to stop acting like an engineer's wet dream and get back into Winnie before a German decides to shoot your too tight ass off."

Alex realized that this wasn't exactly an ideal position and once the weapon was reloaded, she swung around and scampered back into the commander's hatch. Plugging back into the intercom, she asked Becky, "Did she really say all that?"

"Well I might have added a bit, but she did tell me to get you back into Winnie," replied Becky.

Switching back to the platoon net, she heard the Lieutenant repeat, "I repeat all walkers turn and engage the zombies. We need to get them cleared out. Winnie take #2 section down the south flank, I'll take #3 down the north. I hope no one else but Sergeant Mackenzie believes that they can fight the enemy outside their walker.

"No Ma'am," came the chorus of replies from the Guardians.

"Good. Now attack," said the officer.

"Chantal, turn Winnie around and prepare to start working our way back down the line."

"Yes Alex," was the driver's reply.

"What do we have loaded Sarah?" Alex asked.

"HE, Sergeant," replied the gunner.

"Excellent, as soon as Chantal gets us turned around; target the group that I'm putting the tracer into.

With that, the Seaforth Highlanders of Canada's walkers turned around and started their counter attack against the German zombie assault. Winnie advanced slowly putting HE shot into the outer edge of the Zombie line in the hopes of minimizing Canadian casualties. Each shell caused several of the German reanimated dead to be flung off their feet. Sometimes the corpses stayed down, unfortunately most of the time they got back up and continued to move towards the living. That's when the Alex's heavy Browning once again proved its worth. When the gun's heavy rounds hit a zombie, they ripped off limbs and exploded skulls; in other words, the kind of tissue damage even a zombie had difficulty staying mobile with.

Fanning out ahead of Winnie were the two Guardians of #2 Section. Like Winnie, Ida's walker Tony, and Cindy's Lancelot were also armed with 50 calibre Brownings, and these along with their flamethrowers were able to make short work of many zombies. Unfortunately, the light walkers had already been heavily engaged with the German defences and therefore had used up much of their ammunition.

This soon left them with only their 30 calibre Browning and their fists as their only drawn out combat weapons. Both Ida and Cindy decided that their walker's fists were the better, if gorier, choice. They waded into the centre mass of zombies swinging heavy punches and popping zombie heads like too many pimples.

"Hey some of these zombies are wearing brown uniforms," shouted Ida over the platoon network.

"New German uniform?" asked Lieutenant Johnson.

"I don't think so, they're not stylish enough to be German uniforms," replied Ida.

"Sarah, thinks they might be Russian," Becky said over the net.

"Good idea private, but next time go through proper channels, don't just barge in on a conversation above your rank," admonished the Lieutenant.

"If they are Russians, that explains the numbers we're seeing," said Alex.

And they were dealing with a lot of zombies, and the Canadian walkers couldn't be everywhere at once. Fortunately, the column was far from helpless. From inside their Kangaroos the Canadians popped up with Brens, Enfields and every other weapon the infantry had on hand to lay down a line of fire that slowed the undead advance. As well the Alfreds lumbered out of their carriers and started to walk towards the zombies. As they did so the large mechanical infantrymen opened up with their Vickers and Browning machine guns cutting deep into the undead ranks and forcing the remaining German creatures to choose them as target. As the German zombies threw themselves onto Alfreds the robotic infantry's human allies counter attacked. The Canadian infantrymen had found that a sharpened shovel worked best for bashing in a zombie's head. They also found that the undead were nowhere near as scary when they were attacking something else as they were when they were directly attacking you.

So, despite dealing with probably the largest zombie attack on record, the Canadians were holding their own. But in so doing they had to get out of their armoured protection and bunch up. So, when the sound of Moaning Minnies were heard over the battlefield an almost audible groan of frustration could be heard coming from the Canadians.

To make matters worse, the cries of Thors had been well founded. Half a dozen of the large German heavy walkers were advancing up from behind a rise to start raining even more fire onto the support column's exposed personnel. German walker design differed substantially from that of the Western Allies. Whereas the allies had adopted a humanoid appearance for their walker's; the German designs still looked like tanks, only with legs instead of tracks. This gave the large Thors a bloated spider-like appearance, as their Tiger II inspired chassis and turret waddled into position on six large mechanical legs. Armed with a short 150mm howitzer the Thor were designed to destroy infantry, matter how much steel and concrete they were in.

Not caring about their undead troops, the German rockets and artillery shells landed within the column. Infantry, both flesh and steel, were torn apart in the hellfire. Kangaroos and Universal carriers were blasted apart, their armoured frames adding to the metal slashing through the air. Mortar and antitank ammunition from the Seaforth's support company also exploded from near or direct hits from the Thor's cannons; adding to the chaos around them.

The Fort Garry tanks tried to help, responding with their own 76mm canons but the shells just bounced off the front armour of the Thors. A tesla equipped Sherman from the Headquarters platoon, managed to take out one of the monsters with a Rift tech powered blast of manmade lightning: only to be destroyed in turn by a hit from one of the four Zeus class walkers that came lumbering up behind the Thors. These brothers to the Thors look much the same but the howitzer had been replaced by the same 88mm as the King Tiger had. Making them as good as destroying allied armour, as the Thors were at killing infantry.

Both of these German walkers were however, vulnerable to allied walkers when they were crewed by people with guts and experience: which described Winne's crew perfectly.

"Chantal, break right! Make for the corner of the Patherturm position. Get ready for a lateral move right on my command," Alex shrieked over the intercom.

"Roger Alex," shouted back her driver.

"Echo7Alpha this is Echo7Beta, can you hear me?" she said.

There was a short bout of static then Alex heard, "Echo7Beta this is Echo7Alpha I hear you."

Lieutenant Johnson's voice was strained but the relief was palpable.

"Leftenant we need to silence at least one of those Zeues now before they tear through the tanks. I don't have time to describe how we do that. I need you to trust me and follow Winne's lead," Alex said bluntly.

"Go Winnie, Sting will follow your lead," said Lieutenant Johnson, her voice once again calm.

It was then that Alex realized that the Lieutenant hadn't been afraid of the shelling that they were caught up in. She had been scared because she'd not known what to do.

Once they were clear of the artillery blasts, Alex once again popped the hatch on Winnie expecting to be able to grab onto the Browning to steady herself as she talked Chantal through the maneuvers that she intended to put Winnie through. Unfortunately, a piece of shrapnel had sheared the large machine gun off of the walker; costing Alex her most secure hand hold.

"Sarah Load AP, we may only get one shot so it has to count," Alex shrieked over the intercom.

"Confirmed Ma'am," said Sarah who then fired off the 75mm towards the German lines before shouting, "Load AP."

"AP aye," replied Becky.

"Ma'am once you catch up with Winnie, I want you to pop your smoke dischargers," Alex commanded over the platoon net.

"Roger Mackenzie," complied Lieutenant Johnson.

In anticipation of operating mostly in daylight, during the attack, the walker's crews had removed the flare launchers and reinstalled the smoke dischargers. So, when Sting got to Winnies position, they were soon covered by a thick bank of chemical smoke.

"Okay from here it gets tricky. We're going to run in a straight line until we're in line with the nearest Zeus's side armour. From there we move as quickly as possible to get into hand-to-hand range. The legs of these heavy walkers are the weak spot so rip them off and pull it over. At this range a shot from your cannon may penetrate their armour but don't count on it. Instead use it like the world's largest door knocker. We want their attention and to have them traverse their guns at us and away from everyone else," Alex hurried explained.

"That doesn't sound that safe Sergeant," was the Lieutenant's reply.

"They can't lower their guns enough to hit us when we're up that close," replied Alex with confidence.

"Oookay," Lieutenant Johnson said, not quite believing the Sergeant at that point.

"One last thing. When you see Winnie, break left or right go the opposite direction. Lateral movement is our biggest advantage on not getting hit," Alex said before she got ready to charge forward.

"Roger that," was all the Lieutenant said.

Then taking a deep breath Alex turned her attention back to her front and switched her radio back to the intercom setting. "Alright Chantal flank speed forward."

# Chapter Seven: Where Only the Gods Walk

By the time Winnie had cleared the smoke screen he was moving at flank speed and Alex was only able to keep her position by bracing both her arms and legs against the movement.

Looking up she kept an eye on both the nearest Thor and Zeus, watching to see where their turrets were pointed. The Thor appeared to be ignoring them as it continued to fire towards the Canadians' positions. The Zeus on the other hand had seen them and was rotating not only its turret but its entire spider-like body towards them. The German walker's turret was almost in line with Winnie.

"Break right!" ordered Alex.

Winnie suddenly stopped so hard it would have face planted into the ground if Chantal hadn't extended his arms forward to break the fall.

Boom!

The ground to the right of the walker erupted as the shot missed. The Zeus's gunner had of course been leading Winnie, not expecting it to come to such a sudden stop.

Chantal then used Winnies arms to push the Walker back up. Once upright she started Winnie to 'skip' right in a lateral movement throwing the aim of both the Zeus's turret mounted 88 and the bow mounted 20mm autocannon further off.

After moving laterally for some twenty yards Alex ordered "Flank ahead."

Once again, the walker quickly changed directions and sped off quicker than the German gunner could track. Finally, when it was roughly in line with the German Zeus's side, Alex shouted "Pivot!"

Slower than before, so that it didn't risk face planting, Winnie stopped and rotated towards the German heavy walker. Then opening him up once again Chantal had Winnie running towards the Zeus.

As they charged forward the Zeus's bow 20mm finally caught up with Winnie and peppered him with 20mm shells. While they created a holy racket inside the walker, none of the shells had enough power to penetrate.

The main gun however; was almost in position to fire before Winnie could get below its depression.

"Break left! Break left" shouted Alex frantically as she watched the 88 begin to line up with what seemed to be her head.

Looking through her view port Chantal also saw the large gun starting to point at her. Without even stopping she threw Winnie into a lateral move left. In the hands of a lesser skilled driver such a maneuver would have caused the walker to trip over its own feet, or worst break something in the Grizzly's knee or ankle joints. But Chantal was up to the challenge and the girls' hours of maintenance on the walker meant that Winnie's joints held: this time.

The same could not be said for Alex however. She hadn't been expecting the move and the young sergeant had been sent crashing into her hatch. She hissed in pain as she felt at least one of her ribs break; but she was still alive which was more than she could have said otherwise as the 88 shell whizzed by close enough for her to feel the wash.

"Punch it Chantal," shouted Alex through gritted teeth. Once again, the walker started to move forward targeting the closest Zeus which was now frantically trying to get its turret gun aligned with Winnie again. But Winnie won the race and got under the depression of the weapon and next to the heavy walker's left front leg.

Before Alex could even order the attack, Chantal had Winnie's fists starting to smash into the Zeus's knee joint. The first series of blows bent the armour, popping welds, providing Winnie with a hand hold. With the whine of hydraulics Winnie ripped the sheet of armoured plate off of the Zeus's leg exposing the delicate working underneath. Using the armour plate like a giant chisel Winnie smashed open the hydraulic lines; hot oil sprayed out into the air covering both walkers and Alex with an oily film.

Losing power, the leg buckled under its own weight. The large spider-shaped walker should have lurched over to one side, but it too had a good pilot who had already compensated for the loss of that leg and so kept his walker upright. Planting its left centre leg firmly it used that as a pivot point to keep rotating its body in the hopes that Winnie would follow and come into the line of fire of the other German walkers.

However, Winnie wasn't alone; Sting had also made it to the side of Zeus as well and it had been busy smashing its rear leg, quickly disabling it.

"Sarah put the AP round into the centre leg. Chantal rotate so she can get the shot," Alex shouted over the intercom.

Winnie lurched around so that his cannon could fire. The shot, despite being almost at contact range wasn't an easy one; being too close for sights and involving two moving targets. However, Sarah had practiced experience with such close-range shots and knew how to compensate. As she fired, there was a simultaneous shriek of metal as the capped armour piercing round succeeded in punching through the armoured plate protecting the leg to crunch deep into the mechanics.

Switching to the platoon net Alex shrieked into the microphone "Sting! Pull on your leg! Let's get this thing on its side."

Without even responding, Sting started to pull on the rear leg, as Winnie worked on the front. Soon the Zeus's centre leg crumpled and becoming unbalanced the large walker toppled over on its side. The 88 which had been rotating to the side in a vain hope of being able to get a shot at one of the Grizzly walkers was driven into the ground. For several seconds it appeared as if the barrel would keep the large walker in a semi upright position. Then with a groan of bending metal, the Zeus continued over onto its side: hitting the ground with a very satisfying thump.

"Load AP Sarah we're going to snipe at the other walkers while using this one for cover," Alex ordered over the intercom. Then switching to the Platoon net Alex got a hold of Lieutenant Johnson.

"Holy shit! I can't believe we just did that!" was the Lieutenant's reply to the hail.

"Ma'am stay behind the Zeus, and let your gunner snipe at the other Walkers. I'd also suggest getting back to battalion and see if we could get some artillery hitting up here," Alex said with increasing difficulty. Now that the adrenaline of this direct attack was fading the pain of her ribs was starting to make its presence felt.

But as it turned out there was no need for the any artillery attack. Their counterattack had been enough to make the Germans retire. While they only a counted for one walker, the confusion the two of them had caused in the German lines had been enough for the Churchill Meteors to plaster two of the Zeuses with their enzyme rockets putting them out of action. Without their cover, the Thors had been easy meat for the Fort Gary tanks. With a combination of regular armour piercing shot and Tesla created lightning all the remaining Thors were destroyed. The butcher's bill had been high but the 2nd Canadian Brigade had succeeded in punching a hole through the German defences large enough for the 3rd Canadian Brigade to pass through to assault the third defensive belt. After which the armoured division would pass through in exploitation of the breach.

# Chapter Eight: The Bill

They'd done it. They'd breached the Siegfried Line's second defensive belt and fought off the first German counter attack. But right then Alex was in too much pain to care. As the two Seaforth's Grizzlies made their way back to where the bulk of the battalion was deployed, Alex was sitting in her command chair with the blouse of her battle dress around her hips. Becky was standing in her loader's hatch helping Chantal bring Winnie home while Sarah tied a pad around the sergeant's chest to support Alex's broken ribs. This kind of fracture was common among walker crews and all of them knew the proper first aid procedure.

Sarah had wanted to hit Alex with a syrette of morphine but the red-haired sergeant refused.

"I need to stay sharp until we know that we're not needed," Alex explained.

"Right, because being in intense pain helps someone's concentration so much," replied the gunner; disapproval obvious in her voice.

Alex was about to reply when Winnie lurched to one side causing Alex to slam the injured rib into the side of the walker.

"Damnit Chantal you already broke my ribs you can stop trying," hissed Alex in new pain.

"Sorry, we must have a hydraulic leak somewhere in the right leg. It just seized up on me," the driver said.

Getting her blouse at least half back on, Alex gingerly popped her head out of the command hatch. This was where she spent the most time while in Winnie and where she could best ride out Winne's rough trip home.

As they approached their own lines again, she saw that two of the Guardians and a fair number of the automated infantrymen were still moving about the battlefield cleaning up the last of the German Totenkorps. The rest of the battalion got on with the job of opening more lanes through the Dragon's Teeth or setting up defences so that they could hold the position against the German counter attack when it came.

Knowing that Alex wouldn't seek medical attention until she'd reported to the battalion CO Chantal lurched Winnie to what looked to be the Seaforth's forward Headquarters.

As Winnie pulled up next to Sting, Alex saw that the Lieutenant's walker had made it through the attack reasonably intact. There were some deep furrows from where it had taken a burst from a light autogun, but otherwise she still looked battle worthy. The same could be said for her commander. Lieutenant Johnson had already clambered out of her Walker and though she looked paler than usual, everything was still attached.

Gingerly Alex got out of her walker and moved towards where the Lieutenant was currently talking to a medical orderly.

"However, here's one that could use your aide private," Lieutenant Johnson said when she saw Alex.

"I'm healthy enough to report Leftenant," the sergeant said as she attempted to push aside the medical orderly and move to the where she saw the battalion's command staff.

The lieutenant stepped in front of her. "Sergeant Mackenzie you will go with the medical orderly that's an order," Lieutenant Johnson said drawing herself up to her full height.

Then in a much quieter voice she said, "Alex you need to get to the aid station… It's Sergeant Vergamy."

Feeling like she'd just been gut punched, Alex followed the orderly without further protest.

When she got to the aid station she was taken back to where the bodies had been laid out for graves registration to take possession. There she found Ida, resting whole and without a wound yet still under a blanket very dead.

Confused and still in a lot of pain, Alex's tight control broke. She took one of Ida's dead hand into hers and started to weep uncontrollably over her best friend. After a minute she managed to croak out "How?"

"Her walker took a near direct hit from a Thor's heavy howitzer. The armour stopped the shrapnel but the concussion from being so close to the blast…" the orderly couldn't go on.

"She was always giving me a bad time about taking too many risks and this happens," replied Alex. She then fell back into silence.

How long she knelt there holding her dead friend's hand Alex didn't know. Time stopped for her and only restarted when she felt two hands on her shoulders. Looking up she saw Lieutenant Johnson looking down at her with a mixture of concern and sympathy. Behind her was the rest of Winnie's crew with the same looks upon their faces.

"Get her up, and out of here before Steves or another hard ass sees her. The Colonel's left an armoured truck nearby. Get her in the back of it and don't let her leave until she's under control of herself again," ordered the Lieutenant to the rest of Winnie's crew.

"We've got this Leftenant," said Chantal as she helped Alex to her feet.

The four women left as Lieutenant Johnson intimidated the orderly to silence regarding what he had just seen. It didn't take much intimidating: the medical orderly had seen a lot of soldiers break down and as far as he was concerned what happened in the aid station stayed in the aid station.

Once they were in the truck the crew of Winnie just let Alex cry herself out. It took ten minutes but eventually the Sergeant was back in control of herself. Alex then looked at the rest of Winnie's crew with a look of horror on her face.

Understanding her look Becky spoke up "Don't worry, one slip up showing us that you are in fact human isn't going to stop us from knowing that you could kick all of our asses anytime you wanted to."

Alex started to laugh at that but stopped when her broken ribs reminded her that she was still injured. Seeing her grimace in pain Sarah handed Alex a wet cloth to clean up with and then got up and quickly looked out the back of the truck.

"Right the coast is clear, let's get the Sergeant into the battalion aid station to get her ribs looked after," she said to the group.

\*\*

From the Headquarters tent Lieutenant Johnson watched as the crew of Winnie got their now composed sergeant out of the back of the battalion's armoured command truck and to the front of the battalion aid station. While she believed that Sergeant Mackenzie's paranoia about all males in the army was just that, paranoia. The British female officer was willing to admit that there were enough Major Steves out there that caution had to be used.

Fortunately, there were also plenty of men like Lieutenant Colonel Goodbar, and, she believed, Brigadier Sharpe out there. Men who looked to results first and gender second. The integration of women into combat roles was as dependent on men such as these as it was on the women who stepped up to fill those roles.

"Everything alright Leftenant?" asked a voice behind her.

Startled, the young woman quickly turned to come face to face with the commander of the Canadian Seaforths. "Yes sir, thanks to your help, I believe everything will be fine," replied Lieutenant Johnson.

"Sergeant Mackenzie has good instincts. I trust her opinion, even when it paints me as part of the problem," Lieutenant Colonel Goodbar said. He then looked Johnson directly in the eyes and said "Your Grace."

The young woman's guts dropped upon hearing those words. Even though it wasn't the 'proper' form of address, it was clear that Lieutenant Colonel Goodbar knew who she was.

"Who told you?"

"Major Conner, Blastford's liaison officer, let the cat out of the bag when we saw you following Mackenzie on that death or glory attack. He turned paler than the zombies we were dealing with and demanded that I recall you. I refused at first and it was only when he said who you actually were that I was willing to consider this request. But by that time, you two were committed to the attack and it was safer to let you finish than recall you."

Johnson sighed and said, "My father was at Jutland and no one got bent out of shape about that. That's why I'm using the same last name as he did."

"I'm sure someone in his chain of command did get bent out of shape, and besides you can't blame Conner. If you'd been wounded or even worse killed, he would have been the messenger of that piece of unwelcome news. By the way how in the hell did this FUBAR of a situation come about anyways?" Goodbar asked with genuine curiosity.

"A case of the right hand not knowing what the left was doing. The maintenance battalion I was a part of was one of the ones tapped for female walker volunteers. I took the opportunity to volunteer and then made a mad dash to the powers that be to convince them it was a good idea before my opponents could bend their ear with their opposition," explained the young woman.

"Sounds like you're a born walker commander," said the Lieutenant Colonel with a laugh.

"I know the importance of moving at speed when the situation calls for it," Johnson replied. "So now what?"

"A lot of this is beyond my pay grade thankfully. To keep this from blowing up and embarrassing the high command I'll have to downplay you and the Sergeant's actions in the after-action report. I'm willing to do that: for now. But I will not allow your situation from impeding Sergeant Mackenzie and her crew's advancement or from receiving the accolades that they deserve in the long run."

"Don't worry sir, the Sergeant will get everything she deserves, my father can be very persuasive with the General Staff when he wants to be," said the young Lieutenant with a grim smile.

## About the Author

Sandy Addison has always been a story teller; either in the real-world or at the role-playing table. However, it has been only the past few years that he's gained the courage to actually share his stories with others. He's also a great fan of World War II wargames. Thanks to an email to Clockwork Goblin he's gotten the chance to combine his two passions together.

# Other books by this author

Please visit your favorite ebook retailer to discover other books by Sandy Addison:

**The Red Death series**
Sellswords
Children of the Plague (Fall 2020)

**Konflict '47**
Counterattack
Seaforth's Ladies audio format available
Seaforth's Ladies Revised Edition
Going Dutch (Winter 2020)

# Connect with Sandy Addison

Favorite my Smashwords author page:
https://www.smashwords.com/profile/view/Sandy42
Check me out on Goodreads here:
https://www.goodreads.com/author/show/17023729.Sandy_Addison

Made in the USA
San Bernardino, CA
08 July 2020